"If We Wed, It'll Be
A Real Marriage,"

Skye said. "The will calls for a true union in *every* sense of the word."

"I don't think that means—"

"Yes, it does. It means we sleep together."

Flushing slightly, Holly said, "I'm not familiar with *your* personal habits, but *mine* do not include getting into bed with strangers."

"Neither do mine. What I propose is this—we marry as quickly as possible, we live together as the will demands. Separate bedrooms, at the start. We'll get to know each other." He smiled at her. "I'll court you."

She looked away and stared into the fire. She said nothing.

"I'm not going to force myself on you," he went on. "But I do want you, Holly. I won't deny it. I'm not going to hound you, but I will pursue you. Eventually, I hope, I'll wear you down."

Dear Reader,

Let's talk about summer—those wonderful months of June, July and August, when the weather warms up and Silhouette Desire stays hot.

June: Here is where you'll find another dynamite romance about the McLachlan brothers—this time Ross—by BJ James (look for more brothers later in the year!), a *Man of the Month* by Barbara Boswell, and another installment in the *Hawk's Way* series by Joan Johnston.

July: Don't look now but it's the *Red, White and Blue* heroes! These men are red-blooded, white-knight, blue-collar guys, and I know you'll love all of them! Look for the hero portrait on each and every one of these books.

August: It's a *Man of the Month* from Diana Palmer, a story from Dixie Browning and another delightful tale from Lass Small . . . and that's just a *tiny* amount of what's going on in August.

Yes, I think summer's going to be pretty terrific, and in the meantime I want to ask you all some questions. What do you think of the Desire line? Is there anything you'd particularly like to see that we don't provide? No answer is too outrageous; I *want* to hear your opinions.

So write and let me know. And yes, I really do exist! I'm not just some made-up name that goes on the bottom of these letters.

Until next month, happy reading,

Lucia Macro
Senior Editor

LINDA BARLOW
HUNTER'S BRIDE

SILHOUETTE *Desire*

™ Published by Silhouette Books New York

America's Publisher of Contemporary Romance

SILHOUETTE BOOKS
300 East 42nd St., New York, N.Y. 10017

HUNTER'S BRIDE

ISBN: 0-373-05788-1

First Silhouette Books printing June 1993

All the characters in this book have no existence outside the imagination of the author and have no relation whatsoever to anyone bearing the same name or names. They are not even distantly inspired by any individual known or unknown to the author, and all incidents are pure invention.

Books by Linda Barlow

Silhouette Desire

Midnight Rambler #379
Hunter's Bride #788

Silhouette Intimate Moments

Hold Back The Night #166

LINDA BARLOW

writes in several fields, including historical romance, mainstream fiction and contemporary romance. She's been daydreaming for years about "strong, tender heroes with a piratical gleam in their eyes" and believes she may have known a few of them in her various former lives. Linda lives with her husband and daughter outside Boston, where she spends most of her time reading, writing, riding her bike and running up huge phone bills.

One

The night was magical. The full September moon floated on a sea of wispy clouds that crossed, but did not obscure, its shining face. The breeze was warm and moist, scented with wildflowers and lodgepole pine. Crickets chirped, fireflies danced and the earth beneath the cantering hooves of Skye Rawlins's horse was bursting with all the rich aromas of summer's end.

In the distance he could hear a fairy song, borne on the wind. It emanated from deep in the forest, near, he judged, the spring that marked the boundary between his land and her grandfather's.

He knew he would find her there. Appropriate, he thought wryly. Springs and brooks had been associated with magic and mysticism for centuries. Druids, witches and medicine singers the world over had traditionally practiced their spells in such places, and everything he knew about Tom MacLeish's granddaughter, who had moved in with her ailing grandfather here in Whittier, Montana, a couple of months ago, suggested to Skye that she fancied herself to be one of them.

Holly MacLeish was an herbalist who'd relocated from Sedona, Arizona, New Age Nut capital of the southwest. She'd barely been in residence for a month before notices had begun appearing in town, offering seminars in Nature's Medicine and Forest Folklore and similar sorts of foolishness.

Most folks in Whittier had raised their eyebrows and gone about their business. Here in the old Western town where the rolling prairies meet the Great Divide, you don't ask a lot of questions about people's pasts. But you don't accept them, either, until they prove themselves trustworthy. Skye figured it would be a while before anybody trusted Holly's roots, leaves and barks. They hadn't done much to cure her grandfather. If they had, Skye wouldn't have such a gloomy errand to perform tonight.

"Easy, boy, better not rush," he said to Diablo, his horse, as they descended from the scrub into the woodland and slowed to a trot. Both he and his mount knew the terrain intimately—he'd hunted here since his boyhood—but the night was darker under the thick foliage, and he had to be on the lookout for fallen limbs and low-hanging branches.

Ahead, in a pine grove, he could see the crimson glow of a fire. The singing, or chanting, was louder now. First one voice, clear and sweet, then others joining in. Even though the sound was pleasant, it prickled the hairs on the back of his neck. There was something alien and atavistic about a group of women gathered around a fire at midnight while the full moon—a militantly feminine goddess, he recalled—ruled the heavens above.

"Hope they don't tear us limb from limb, fella," he said to Diablo. "I don't know what the blazes they're up to, but whatever it is, I'll lay you fair odds that males are not invited."

Approaching even more slowly now, Skye tried to make out the words of the women's song. Something about trees and wildflowers, roots, flowers and fruits. The beauty of the earth, cloaked in the green things she brought forth. The loveliness of nature.

Sounds pretty tame, he thought. The rumor around town was that Holly MacLeish and her friends were recklessly invoking the power of the pagan deities who'd inhabited this woodland many thousands of years ago. Some folks, in fact, weren't too happy about it.

"It's devil worship, if you ask me, Sheriff," old Mr. Galleger had complained to Skye. "You ought to do something about it. Last thing we need 'round these parts is a bunch of witches and satanists."

"Easy now, Roy," Skye had protested, "this is Whittier, not Salem."

Skye brought Diablo to a halt within hailing distance of the grove. He could see them clearly now, six women standing in a circle around a small, rock-ringed fire. All except one of them were wearing jeans and T-shirts; she, the leader, was clad in a white peasant blouse and a multicolored skirt that brushed her ankles.

Holly MacLeish. The woman who intrigued him. The woman who'd turned him down. The woman who would only allow him to admire her from afar.

Her midnight-black hair flowed loose and wavy down to the middle of her back. Her face was pure of form and line, its classic beauty marred only by a whimsically upturned nose and the hint of stubbornness in her chin. Her body was slender and graceful. Athletically fit, yet wholly feminine. A gleaming gold belt that resembled a serpent was cinched around her narrow waist, and she wore a bracelet of similar design high on her arm.

Her feet were bare, as were the feet of all the women in the circle. They clearly weren't worried about the poison ivy that was all over the area. They probably spoke to it, he thought wryly, asking it to leave them alone.

The singing had stopped. In a liquid, bell-toned voice, his quarry said, "Blessed be. I'd like to go around the circle now, with each of you describing the healing powers of your own special plant. Please speak as if you *were* the plant. It will make your identification with our herbal sisters stronger and aid your memory in learning. Moira, you've been to one of my seminars before. Would you like to begin?''

A heavyset red-haired woman immediately to Holly's right closed her eyes and intoned, "I am called Mugwort, but I prefer my Latin name, *Artemisia,* named for the great goddess of the moon. I am a magical herb, used in ceremony for millenia, commonly found in fields and sunny places. My leaves are feathery, the undersides a silvery gray, and my flowers are tiny green bells. In addition to my anti-inflammatory qualities, I am beloved of women, for I aid in bringing on the moon time. If you put me under your pillow at night, your dreams will be vivid and prophetic."

Sure, Skye thought. What a crock of shoe shine.

"I am Saint-John's-wort," the next woman began. They had linked hands around the circle and were swaying slightly from side to side while they listened to each other recite. "My starlike yellow flowers brighten the meadows in summer, although your fingers will turn crimson as you harvest me. My flowers make a soothing balm for burns...."

Skye tuned out the botany lecture, refocusing on the gorgeous woodland sprite who had initiated it. Tightening his thighs, he urged Diablo to move closer so he could better regard her intent face, her full lips, her large, luminous eyes. He wanted to absorb every detail, now, before he was forced to confront Holly MacLeish with the reason for his interruption. He wanted to remember her as she was at this moment—silent, dreamy, lovely. Goddess of the night.

At last, like it or not, she was going to have to interact with him. Too bad it was under these circumstances.

Since the first time he'd seen her picking up groceries for her ailing grandfather in the general store, Skye had been strongly drawn to Holly MacLeish. It was the natural response of an unattached male to an attractive single woman . . . at the start, anyway. Skye had always appreciated beautiful women.

Next, they'd had a little set-to over the issue of the fire permit, which the forest rangers hadn't been too eager to grant. Holly had come up with a law in the books from 1888 that allowed the use of properly tended fires for ceremonial purposes, and demanded that Skye, as sheriff, approve her application. He'd done so, taking the opportunity to invite her and her grandfather to come to his place for dinner. Courteously but firmly, she had declined, and Tom had come without her.

His curiosity aroused, Skye had tried again. He'd called her a week or so later with another invitation—lunch this time. With him. Alone.

"No, thank you," she'd replied. "I'm really not interested," she'd said more insistently a couple of weeks later when he'd given it one more shot.

"She's a little shy around men," her grandfather had explained. "Besides, she's got this silly city prejudice against men who enjoy hunting and fishing," he continued. "Especially hunting. 'You certainly can't expect me to be civil toward another man who kills helpless animals for his own pleasure,' she said to me the other day. I told Holly she was gonna have a rough time up here in Montana, finding herself a man who doesn't hunt or fish, but the girl's real stubborn. Doesn't need a man, or so she claims."

"Fine with me," Skye had replied somewhat testily. "Last thing I need is an animal-rights activist."

"I think she even believes in *plant* rights," Tom had said ruefully. "She's always talking to the wretched things."

It was silly, he knew—Skye believed himself to have outgrown this sort of thing years ago—but Holly's hard-to-get routine had intrigued him. She'd become a challenge. He loved a good challenge. Made the adrenaline sing in his veins.

"I am Yarrow," she was saying. All the other women had taken their turn, moving the recitation back around to Holly. "With my tiny white flowers and finely dissected leaves, I am the bloodstancher, the healer of wounds."

He'd heard enough. So had Diablo. Impatient with the inactivity, the stallion shook his head and nickered. Holly MacLeish's rapt expression vanished as her eyelids lifted, and she stared into the shadows beyond her fire. As the women dropped hands and began looking around, Holly raised her voice. "Hello?" There was wariness in her tone. "Is someone out there?"

"I reckon it's time for our grand entrance," Skye said to his horse. Exerting pressure with his knees, he rode into the firelight.

* * *

When first she saw him cloaked in darkness, Holly felt an eerie sense of dislocation, as if the forest were slipping away. For a moment there was nothing but herself and the horseman, meeting somewhere on a treeless, barren plain. A stab of primal terror reverberated through her. Deliberately, she took a deep breath to calm herself.

As the shrouded rider emerged from the woods and approached the fire, it struck her that he seemed larger than life—more myth than man. Clad entirely in black and mounted on a black stallion, he looked like a creature of the night, godlike and powerful, maybe malevolent. The devil himself out to tempt and beguile her.

She shook her head, as if to clear it of such a ridiculous fantasy. But the fear that she persistently attempted to deny was rooted deep inside her. To Holly, the devil was real. Just over a year ago she had been assaulted in her herb shop in Sedona, Arizona, by a man named Willy Hess. He had been stalking her— and terrifying her—for a long time.

Despite a vague resemblance, this shadowy figure couldn't be Willy Hess. Her nemesis was dead.

She stepped forward. She hated feeling the slickness on her palms as she clenched her fists. It infuriated her that she still didn't feel safe after all these months.

"Who are you?" He was still in the darkness; she couldn't see his face. "You frightened us."

"Sorry about that," he said, dismounting and coming into the light.

He was tall, as Willy had been, with broad shoulders and long, muscular arms and legs. The dark clothes, she could see now, consisted of a navy work shirt and black jeans, the lower cuffs pulled down over a pair of slick riding boots. His hair was black, thick, and a shade too long. His face, as the firelight struck it, was handsome, and she finally recognized him.

"You're Sheriff Rawlins," she said, dry-throated but relieved.

"At your service, ma'am," he drawled, smiling, and offered her his hand.

She took it, but was quick to extricate her fingers from his warm, firm grasp. "My neighbor," she explained to her students. "Mr. Rawlins owns the land adjoining my grandfather's. He's also the local long arm of the law."

He was staring at her, so she returned the scrutiny. Regular features, clean lines and angles. Good eyes— large, expressive and direct. A strong blade of a nose over a generous, mobile mouth. A slight cleft in the chin, as if pressed in the womb with a phantom finger. He wore a mustache, black and bushy, which she suspected was a recent addition. He'd been clean shaven in the photograph that her grandfather had sent her a few months ago, when she'd still been living in Arizona. Rawlins and her grandfather, clad in fishing vests and waders, standing in a spring creek and proudly holding up a gigantic rainbow trout.

"What's the problem, Sheriff? Is our chanting disturbing someone? Or it is the matter of the fire again? I assure you, we have a permit." Her tone was cool, although her innate congeniality softened it more than she knew.

When he shook his head, she added, "Could it be that we're interfering with your hunt? I've heard that you ride around the countryside on a black stallion, a shotgun slung across your thighs, just in case you happen to run across any small, defenseless animals."

"And I've heard that you talk to plants," he countered. He glanced significantly around the circle. "I'm curious—do they answer?"

He was mocking her. She felt a twinge of regret for her own rudeness, but she hated hunters. And feared them. Willy Hess had been a hunter.

Holly had never had much patience with the impulse that allows a modern, civilized adult to run around the fields and forests with a shotgun, stalking animals whose meat he did not require for food and whose fur he did not require for warmth. According to Grandpa, Skye Rawlins had worked for a few years in Los Angeles, where he'd been a highly paid attorney. No doubt he'd taken a drastic cut in pay when he'd decided to return to his Montana home and police the area, but he certainly didn't *need* to hunt.

Although she knew her grandfather was fond of Rawlins, Holly had not wished to become better acquainted. In fact, she'd been avoiding him. She was weary of hearing what a good companion he was—he took Grandpa fishing. What a loyal friend—he lent Grandpa money. What an entertaining raconteur—he knew a lot of dirty jokes. What a prodigious intellect—he beat Grandpa at chess.

She didn't believe a word of it. Tom MacLeish was a notoriously bad judge of character. For as long as Holly could remember he had been getting himself cheated, swindled and betrayed by his supposed friends. A cheerful, openhearted man, Grandpa often seemed to her to be a cosmic innocent, wandering through a fallen world whose schemes and deceptions he simply couldn't understand.

He'd been married twice after Holly's grandmother's death; both women had left him for younger, more exciting men. He'd lost most of his life savings a few years ago when a clever con man had talked him into investing in a scorched piece of Nevada desert. Worst of all, he'd trusted the incompetent medical doctor—sued several times for malpractice—who'd assured Grandpa that he didn't need any tests and there was absolutely nothing the matter with him.

The doctor had been wrong. Grandpa had cancer, and he'd suffered for nearly a year before getting treatment. Because of his willingness to believe whatever people told him, Tom MacLeish was dying.

Holly was sure that Rawlins knew this. But it hadn't stopped him from dragging her grandfather out flyfishing in the early hours of the morning or at dusk, after a long day. Grandpa would come in, pale and exhausted, more often than not damp from a leak in his waders. "Skye says trout fishing is good therapy," he would insist.

"Skye Rawlins is an interfering bully who has even less sense than you. You're sick, Grandpa, and he's making you worse!"

"Nonsense. I always feel fine when I'm with him. Skye's a good, decent man, and I'm sure that if you got to know him, you'd like him very much."

Holly had kept her doubts to herself. She'd heard a lot of whispers around town about Skye Rawlins, his past and his present. He was Montana born and bred, and had hightailed it out to the West coast after misspending his youth drinking, joyriding and raising hell. Supposedly he'd straightened out and made something of himself in California, then quit life in the fast lane and come home to Whittier, Montana.

Local tongues were busiest when it came to the rumors about his love life. His determination to remain a free spirit had apparently broken several hearts, which didn't surprise her. With that big, handsome body and that insolent masculine grace, he seemed the type, all right.

"What do you want, Mr. Rawlins?" she asked now. "It's getting late, and we'd like to continue our circle."

"I need to talk to you." He hesitated. "But first, what is this, exactly? A back-to-nature earth goddess thing?"

"I'm an herbalist. I'm running weekend seminars for students while I try to set up a herb farm and a more formal school here in Whittier. My plans are in the preliminary stages at present, and my teaching methods are experimental.''

"So it seems. Most instructors don't hold classes in the woods at midnight. Some folks around town think you're witches. Me, I'm not so superstitious." He smiled as he spoke, and Holly noticed his mouth again—full-lipped and sensuous. She was startled by the thought that zipped through her mind: hunter or no, he's incredibly sexy.

Don't even consider it, she ordered the susceptible female side of herself. That way darkness lies.

In a frosty tone she said, "You still haven't told me why you're here."

His smile faded. "I know. I guess I'm procrastinating." He glanced toward the other women, who seemed to be following the conversation attentively. "I'll need a few minutes alone with you, if you don't mind."

She followed him a few steps away from the rest of the group. "What's so private and important?"

"Look, Holly, I'm afraid it's about your grandfather."

Whatever assurance she'd possessed deserted her. She could feel herself stiffen as her nerves and muscles zinged with anxiety. She had forgotten one of the primary responsibilities of local police and sheriff's departments—to notify relatives of accidents and deaths. "What do you mean? What's happened? Has the hospital been trying to reach me?"

"Yes. When they got no answer, they tried me instead. I guess everyone knows we're neighbors."

"What's the matter with him?" Without conscious awareness of her action, she reached out to steady herself with a grip on his arm. "Oh, God, he's not dead, is he?"

"No, no, he's still alive. But he's taken a turn for the worse. I'm not sure why, exactly. You know how they are about giving out that sort of information over the phone." More gently, he added, "Holly, he's asking for you."

"I'll go at once. I'll hurry back to the house and get the car—"

"No. Listen. I'll take you. You're quite a hike from your place. You're a slender thing, and Diablo will be able to carry us both. It'll be much faster that way."

She cast a doubtful look at the huge black stallion. But it didn't seriously occur to her to refuse. It no longer mattered that Sheriff Skye Rawlins was a bloodthirsty hunter who killed small animals for pleasure. The only thing that mattered now was that he was her grandfather's friend.

"Thank you. I'd appreciate that. Let's go at once." She reached for the horn of Diablo's saddle. "Help me up."

She was groping for the stirrup when she felt his hands encircle her waist and lift. She threw her right leg over and settled awkwardly into the saddle. Skye Rawlins's limbs were much longer than hers so, mounted, she couldn't reach the stirrups.

"Slide forward," he ordered. "This is going to be awkward."

He swung up behind her, letting her have the saddle, reaching around her for the stirrups and reins. Everything felt out of kilter, and Diablo pranced as if he didn't much care for the arrangement. But Rawlins was clearly an experienced rider and the stallion an intelligent horse.

"Holly, what's happening?" one of her students asked.

Briefly, she explained. "Please, Moira, you're the most experienced here. Will you take the others back to the house?"

"Of course," the heavyset woman said. "I'm so sorry. Don't worry about anything here."

"Thanks." She turned her attention to Skye. "Come on. What are we waiting for?"

"Have you done much riding?"

"Hardly any, I'm sorry to say."

"You just mounted an oversized stallion without an ounce of hesitation," he said, all trace of mockery gone from his voice. "I admire your guts."

"Don't. I'm terrified." She was clutching the saddle horn so tightly, her knuckles threatened to break through her skin.

"Relax." He slipped one arm around her waist and moved in a little closer to her body. "I'll keep you safe."

She tried not to stiffen from the sudden intimate contact with a stranger; she didn't want to insult him when he was doing his best to be of assistance. But she could hardly help being aware of him. There was something surreal about the situation. Dreamlike. He was an attractive man. He had asked her out several times, invitations she had firmly declined, yet now he was holding her in his arms. Frightened though she was for Grandpa, she could not deny how exciting—and terrifying—it felt to be seated astride Skye Rawlins's coal-colored stallion, feeling his arm circling her waist, his thighs locked around her bottom and his hard belly against her back.

They set off at a brisk walk. "I won't let you fall," he assured her as her knuckles turned even whiter.

"I'm not worried about falling. I'm worried about my grandfather. Can't we go any faster?"

He tightened his knees on Diablo's flanks and urged him on until the trees melted into a blur.

He was nothing more than a vehicle to her, he knew. But for him, from the moment he'd touched her, everything in his life had shifted and changed. She was everything he'd dreamed she'd be. Her slim body so close to his made him dizzy. Her hair, flowing like black silk down to the middle of her back, smelled fresh and clean and faintly exotic. Herbs, he thought, wishing he could bury his face in it. Wishing he could bury his face in *her*.

Shame needled him. Here he was, fixating on this woman, reveling in the lust and desire she had unknowingly aroused in him at the same time that Tom MacLeish, her grandfather and his friend, was fighting for his life in the hospital.

No good can come of this, he thought.

Two

They were talking about hunting. Or rather, Skye Rawlins was talking and Grandpa was listening, his frail fingers tight on the hospital sheet, his eyes intent on his friend's face.

"There's nothing like it. Rising before the dawn to dress in the dark, dragging on those heavy socks and long undies to keep warm even though you're toasting in your country kitchen with the bacon frying on the stove and the coffee bubbling in the pot, and you're too revved up with anticipation to care about the cold outside, the bone-stiffening chill in the crisp autumn air.

"You've got your dogs, rushing about underfoot, eager to go, sensing the joy of the chase. You've got your orange cap and comfy old shooting vest and your shell boxes and shotguns—the new double you bought last winter as well as the trusty old single shot your dad gave you on your twelfth birthday. That old gun takes you back to those days when you were young and short of leg, too new-hatched to drink the coffee that the men gulped to keep warm, too shy and too dumb to have an opinion on whether or not that thorny blowdown over there might be sheltering grouse.

"Those days were magical, those golden mornings when leaves crunched underfoot and the skeleton limbs of the trees scratched the pale blue of the November sky and the woods went on forever. Those were the days when we learned to love the land and all its miraculous creatures."

"Used to hunt with my dad," Grandpa whispered. "Down near Yellowstone. Wilderness all around in those days, but now it's ski lodges and time-shares all over the place."

"Same everywhere," Rawlins agreed. "Construction where the woods used to be, rivers and streams that are losing fish, dying of pollution. 'Course, it's worse in the cities. I spent the past few years in god-awful L.A., where it's drugs that get hunted, and teenage kids."

"The world's changed." His voice was very low; the words came hard. "Don't like what it's becoming. Guess I won't mind leaving it."

"That's enough of that kind of talk."

Rawlins was seated on a folding chair pulled up beside Tom's bed, just opposite from the window where

Holly was pacing back and forth. He'd driven her to the hospital in Bozeman and stayed with her ever since. It was now the middle of the night; she had lost track of the exact time. Grandpa was in intensive care, hooked up to all sorts of machines, suffering from symptoms that had little or nothing to do with his cancer. He'd had a massive heart attack. The prognosis was not good.

The nursing staff had tried to convince them to leave, but Holly was afraid Grandpa wouldn't last the night. Skye Rawlins had taken the shift supervisor aside for a chat, and she'd agreed to let Holly stay for as long as she liked. Rawlins seemed to feel this meant that he could stay, as well.

He must want something. Why else would he be so devoted to his eccentric elderly neighbor?

What he wants, she thought wryly, is me. He'd tried to date me and I'd said no. That was probably all it took to whet the appetite of a lady-killer like Skye Rawlins, with his strong, well-exercised body, his lazy smile and his big, blue, come-into-my-parlor eyes.

Oh, stop being so cynical, she chided herself. He's a kind man, behaving like a concerned friend and neighbor. My goodness, it's about time you stopped being so skittish around men.

Still, it seemed reasonable that she should be suspicious of Skye Rawlins's motives. Not long ago Grandpa had said something about selling him a chunk of land. "I need the money," he'd told her. "Hate to do it—the land's been in the family for so many generations—but Skye wants it bad, and he's the one man I could sell to without regret. I know he won't parcel it off to one of those Yuppie resort developers who've been hanging about lately. Skye loves the land."

"What he loves is any bird or animal he can murder on the land. Don't even think of selling to him, Grandpa. I have some money from Dad's life insurance. I can help out."

"Can't take your money, pumpkin," he'd insisted. "You'll need it in the years ahead. Besides, it isn't enough."

"What do you mean, it isn't enough? How big are your debts?"

He'd refused to tell her. "A man's debts are his own private business," was all he would say. "Don't worry about it. I've got it covered."

What if Skye's presence here tonight had nothing to do with his amorous inclinations and everything to do with the land? *Skye wants it bad*. Was this his last chance to scavenge something from her grandfather before he died? She half expected him to pull out a briefcase and shove some papers under Grandpa's nose for his signature. He was an attorney, after all, even if he wasn't currently practicing.

Looking at the two of them, Skye's dark, handsome face inclined toward Grandpa's pathetically thin and sunken visage, it was hard to believe that he could have any ulterior motives. Would I be so suspicious of him, she asked herself, if the tall, dark-haired man who assaulted me in Sedona hadn't borne a vague resemblance to Skye Rawlins?

As if he felt Holly's gaze upon him, Skye looked up. Grandpa's eyes had closed; he seemed asleep. But Skye was alert and wary. The corners of his mouth stiffened as their eyes met. In that moment he seemed to see into her soul. She felt naked, embarrassed. She felt the way a deer must feel when it looked up and saw him aiming down the barrel of a shotgun.

Skye Rawlins was not Willy Hess. But Holly had the uncanny sense that he was going to do something, somehow, to hurt her.

Skye was thinking that this was not going as well as he'd hoped. She didn't like him. He wondered why. A few weeks ago she'd refused a date with a stranger, but he'd figured that once she got to know him, she'd come around.

My male arrogance, he thought wryly. Serves me right.

But in recent years, it seemed, he'd rarely had to chase women. They came after him. According to the experts, there was no mystery about this. It was all a matter of demographics. There were more single women in the thirty to forty age group than single men. Combine that with the way guys his age tended to date younger women and you had a lot of thirty-something females eagerly competing for a smaller number of flattered but befuddled males.

Back in the wild days of his youth, Skye had enjoyed doing the chasing. But he knew he'd be accused of sexism nowadays if he admitted that he'd still rather be the one to make the phone calls, plan the evening, pay for the dinner, initiate the sex. Seduction was not as much fun, he'd decided, when you were always the one being seduced.

No danger of that here. He knew the subtle signals, the unspoken cues. She wasn't interested. Period.

She had been courteous but distant. After that fleeting few minutes of physical proximity on horseback when his arms had been hard around her and her heartbeat had blended with his own, she had withdrawn into herself again. His instincts warned that this was a woman you could get only so close to. Push her and she'd slip away.

Most women say the same thing about me, he reminded himself. He'd never scored too high on any girlfriend's intimacy scale.

Still, he wished he knew more about Holly. Her father, Tom's son, had been killed twenty years ago in an auto accident. Holly had been a child then. Was there a mother somewhere? What about men? She hadn't married, but there must have been lovers in her life. Where were they now? Why was this lovely, black-haired woman alone?

Tom MacLeish groaned in his sleep, sending a renewed stab of shame through Skye. His physical response to Holly kept distracting him from the reason they were here. What the hell could he expect from her under these circumstances? She was focused entirely on her grandfather. And rightly so. Only a miserable, heartless, hormone-drenched wretch like himself would be sitting here estimating his chances of mak-

ing it with Tom's granddaughter while Tom himself
was lying in front of him, dying.

The worst of it was, he and Tom were good friends.
There was something sweet and calm about Tom's
personality that had provided an anchor for Skye in
the difficult months of readjusting to a quiet life in the
Montana wilderness. Tom had been someone to talk
to, someone to fret about, someone who was there to
relieve the worst crush of his loneliness after he'd decided to quit his rat-race existence in L.A.

Tom MacLeish was a man's man, which had been
just what he'd needed. He'd understood Skye's desire
for solitude and independence; he'd never come too
close nor demanded too much. He'd known and respected the boundaries of intimacy. Women couldn't
do that. They couldn't back off, leave you alone. They
didn't seem to understand the basic premise of masculine friendship—you were there for your friend if he
needed you. But you preferred that he relied on himself. Which, nine times out of ten, he did.

When a man was dying, though, he counted on his
buddies to do whatever had to be done. Skye was
willing. To him it was a point of honor: you stood up
for your friends.

You also stood up for their lovely, raven-haired
granddaughters, if such was the task to which you
were called. Even if they did look at you as if they
suspected you might be every bit as vicious as some of
the criminals you used to defend.

Tom shifted in bed. Once again, he opened his eyes.
"Holly?"

Skye's throat ached when he saw Holly's face brighten. She was hoping he was going to make it. Losing him was going to be tough.

"Love you, lassie," Tom whispered. His breathing, Skye noted, was much more labored now. Holly must have noticed it, too, because the spark of hope in her eyes faded and tears began streaming down her cheeks.

"I love you, too," she said, taking a tight grip of her grandfather's fragile fingers. Skye knew she was holding on to more than just his hands. She was trying to stay the flight of his soul.

MacLeish's expression had changed from peaceful to frantic. "Holly? Promise me."

"What, Grandpa? What do you want me to promise?"

"That you'll...abide by my wishes. That you won't—" he broke off to cough "—won't...challenge my will."

"Of course not, Grandpa. Don't worry about that. But we won't need your will for a good long time. You're doing fine. Please keep hanging on."

Why should she challenge his will? Skye wondered. He couldn't imagine that there could be much to challenge. Tom owned several hundred acres of rugged back country—some of which Skye had hoped to acquire for himself since it adjoined his own smaller property—but there wasn't much money. He knew this because Tom had hit him for several substantial loans. Which reminded him, he'd better remember to tear up the paperwork. He didn't want Holly to get stuck with repaying him; she would have little enough as it was.

"Everything I've done, I've done for you," breathed Tom. "You won't understand it, you probably won't like it, but one day things'll come right, and then you'll see."

"I know that, Grandpa." She leaned over to kiss his brow. "You've been so good to me, always, and I love you very much."

"Then promise me that you'll abide by my wishes as stated in my letter. That you won't challenge my will."

"Uh, what letter, Grandpa?"

He coughed, badly this time. When he could speak, he whispered, "Say it, Holly. Please."

Holly looked over at Skye with raised eyebrows, apparently seeking advice. He wished he could give it to her, but he had no idea what Tom was talking about. He shrugged his shoulders and showed her his hands, palms up.

"Holly?"

Leaning over, she gently kissed her grandfather's sunken cheek. "I promise I'll abide by your wishes as stated in your letter and I won't challenge your will," she stated in a firm, clear voice.

Tom sank back, obviously relieved. "You're a good girl, Holly. Always were. I'm just trying to—to take care of you." His eyes wandered. "Is Rawlins there? I want . . . must talk to him, too."

Skye joined her by the side of the bed. "I'm here, Tom. Shoot."

"You, too, lad. Promise me."

"Sure. What?"

"The same."

"You want me to make sure everything's in order with your will? I'm not your lawyer. But I'll check up on whoever is and make sure your wishes are respected, if that's what you're worried about."

Grandpa was shaking his head. "You're not my lawyer, I know," he said in a stronger voice. "But you can make a verbal contract, can't you? One you'll swear to honor?"

"I can make a promise. I think you know me well enough to be sure that I never break my word."

"Then say it. Promise you'll abide by the wishes stated in my letter. And you won't challenge my will."

"Tom, your will isn't my concern. But as an attorney, I can certainly advise Holly, if that's what you—"

"It *is* your concern," Grandpa barked at him. "Promise me."

"Okay," he said, shrugging. His eyes met Holly's. She nodded, encouraging him. "I'll abide by your wishes. I won't challenge your will or let anybody else do so. You have my word. Rest easy now, Tom. I'll take care of everything. And I'll watch out for your granddaughter for you, so don't worry about that."

Grandpa smiled. He relaxed visibly. "Love you," he murmured. "Love you both."

It was as if the effort to extract the promises had been the last thing that had kept him animated, and there was nothing further to be said or done. Closing his eyes, he nodded once and let the breath ease out of him in a gentle sigh. He did not breathe again.

"Grandpa?" Holly whispered. "Grandpa!"

Nothing. Tom MacLeish's face seemed to settle into an expression of peacefulness so deep and so pure that Skye felt a moment of awe. Death did not frighten him, and he sensed that Holly felt no fear of it, either. Working close to nature as she did, close to the earth, she probably regarded it as a natural process, part of the inevitable cycle of life. Not that this made mortality any easier to accept. He saw her shudder and knew how fiercely she must resent death's power to separate her from the people she loved.

"Oh, Skye, he's gone." She whispered the words as if that would make them less real.

He moved closer, allowing his hands to settle onto her shoulders. As soon as he touched her, she crumpled. He caught her, turned her, supported her, felt the mettle inside her gather and reform. She regained her balance but remained in his arms, shivering slightly, the tears chasing each other down her cheeks.

"I'm sorry, Holly. He was a good man."

"There's nobody like him." Her voice was muffled against his neck; he could feel the warmth of her breath. "When I was a teenager, he saved my sanity. Maybe my life. I owe him everything. And I loved him so much."

"He loved you, too." Her sanity? Maybe her life? What had happened to her? he wondered. She intrigued him.

"I miss him already."

"I know." Skye stroked her shoulders and back, feeling the subtle musculature under the skin. She was slender but strong. Her body was beautiful. "Me, too."

Somewhere an alarm was sounding—the cardiac monitor must have touched it off. Skye noted the commotion in the hallway, saw the hurried entrance of a doctor and a nurse. Not a damn thing they could do now.

They stood together in their sad embrace. She grieved while he tried his best to console her with his energy and vitality. She shifted, and Skye thought he felt her mouth brush his throat. The desire to gather her closer, kiss her, soothe her, touch her all over nearly overwhelmed him. But he knew she had no awareness of anything that he was feeling, so caught up was she in her own loss.

She broke free, turned back to the bed and lightly stroked her grandfather's chiseled face. Ignoring the doctors and nurses who were crowding around, she bent and touched her lips to his closed eyes. "Goodbye, Grandpa," she murmured, her voice broken. "Blessed be."

"I'll watch out for her, Tom," Skye repeated under his breath.

Three

———

"You can't be serious," Holly said. "This is impossible."

She was sitting in the Bozeman office of Meyer, Bolton and Brannen, her grandfather's attorneys, listening to the reading of his will. Skye Rawlins was sitting beside her, having been asked to attend by the lawyers. She had thought this odd, but she now understood.

"Are you telling me that my grandfather has divided the property? That he's left all the land to Sheriff Rawlins and only the house to me?"

Looking uncomfortable, Geoffrey Bolton, a dour, middle-aged man in an ill-fitting suit and a hairpiece, met her eyes briefly. "The house and all its furnishings and personal items, yes. And the barn. In addition to the half acre of land the buildings sit on. The remainder of the property goes to Mr. Rawlins."

"There has to be some mistake," she said, rising. "I saw my grandfather's will. Skye Rawlins was not named. Why would he be? He's not a member of the family."

"This is a new will, dated less than three weeks ago."

Skye was on his feet, also. "If Tom made a new will in my favor, he must have been mentally impaired during the last few weeks of his life. It'll never stand up."

"I executed the will myself," said Geoffrey Bolton. "I've known Tom for years. He knew exactly what he was doing."

"That can't be—"

"If you will just be patient, Ms. MacLeish, you will hear that there are some conditions attached to the will. But before getting to those, I'd like to read a letter that will explain Tom's intentions. The matter is rather complicated, not to mention highly unusual, but he was an unusual man, as you know."

"Look, Bolton, I'm not taking his land away from his only grandchild," Skye said. He stalked back and forth before adding, "It's my understanding that Holly is starting an herb business in Whittier, or a school or something. She'll need the land."

"It's more than that. I love the land. I grew up here. It's part of me. My grandfather knew that. I can't believe he would do such a thing. It's inconceivable."

"Holly will challenge the will, of course, and I won't stand in her way," Skye said. "As a matter of fact—" He stopped.

As their eyes met, Holly knew what he was thinking. The realization had struck her, as well. She envisioned Grandpa, struggling for breath, insisting on her promise...on Skye's..."My God. We told him we wouldn't challenge."

"Yeah, I know, but—"

"We also promised to abide by the wishes in his letter, whatever they are."

"We were humoring a dying man, for heaven's sake."

Stunned, she shook her head. Grandpa knew how she felt about promises. Everybody has a few values in life that they believe in absolutely. Holly believed in keeping her word. She and Grandpa had discussed it often. You didn't deliberately hurt someone, you didn't betray a friend, and you didn't break your promises. It was the same, she suspected, with Skye Rawlins. *I think you know me well enough to be sure that I never break my word.*

"Blast him, the old son of a gun," Rawlins muttered. He slammed one fist into his other palm. "So this is what he was up to."

"Apparently so. But I still don't understand, I don't see why—"

"Let's hear the damn letter."

The attorney cleared his throat noisily before beginning. "I'd appreciate it if you would both restrain any outbursts until I get to the end."

"That bad, huh?" said Skye.

His expression determinedly neutral, Geoffrey Bolton began to read.

"My Dear Ones,

"By now you both will have heard the contents of my will. I imagine you're confused and defiant, wondering what the hell that crazy old man is thinking of. Bear with me, please. I have a plan.

"Holly, you're my only living relation and I love you more than I can possibly express. But I haven't done well by you. All the money I've ever had has slipped right through my fingers. But the worst of it is, since I've been sick, *other* people's money has also slipped away. If it were not for the friend who's lent me far more than I could ever hope to replay, I'd have been tossed out of house, home and hospital long ago.

"Holly, my benefactor is Skye Rawlins. He's a good man, and I owe him. I can't, in honor, die without repaying my debt to him. It would be a betrayal of friendship, and you know how I feel about that.

"That's why I'm leaving him the land. He wants it, he loves it, and the good Lord knows, he's lent me more than it's worth. It's all I have to give.

"I know you love it, too, Holly. And I know you were hoping to set up your herb school here. I'd like you still to be able to do that. But I worry that if left to your own devices, you'll continue to surround yourself with your crazy feminist friends—herbalists and trance channelers and goddess worshippers and New-Age witches—and you'll never let a single member of the opposite sex near the place.

"You're nearly thirty and, as far as I can tell, there's no romance in your life. You and I both know why. But this can't continue, Holly. You can't judge the whole male sex by the viciousness of one of its members.

"As for you, Skye, much though you might deny it, I suspect what you really want is to put aside your wild ways, find your roots and establish a family. I know you're cynical about the possibilities, but hell, why else do you suppose you decided to come home to Montana?

"The two of you have a lot in common. More than you know. You'll thank me one day.

"That's all I've got to say. Bolton will explain the conditions of my will. I charge you both to respect the wishes of a dying man.

"That's how the letter ends," Geoffrey Bolton said. "He signs it with his love."

Holly said nothing. Anger had risen up at several points in the letter—particularly during his remarks about her lack of a love life and her crazy feminist friends—but even more powerful was the sorrow that choked her at hearing the familiar cadences of her grandfather's words and phrases. During the years she'd lived in Arizona, Grandpa had written to her often. She'd loved receiving his rambling letters. It was impossible to believe that he would never write again.

"This is beginning to sound ominous to me," Skye said. "You'd better explain the conditions, Bolton."

The lawyer coughed. His eyes darted about, seemingly eager to fix on anything other than their faces. "Very well. You get the land, Sheriff, but only if you agree to, uh, marry Ms. MacLeish immediately and maintain a joint residence in the house for a minimum period of six months."

"Marry me?" Holly yelled.

Skye's comment would have resulted in a contempt of court citation had he uttered it in front of a judge.

"The marriage must be a true union in every sense of the word," Bolton added. "It can be dissolved only in the case of irreconcilable differences. If, in other words, you and Ms. MacLeish cannot tolerate each other's company, you may divorce after the six-month cohabitation, at which point the property, house and land, will be equally divided between you in any manner that is agreeable to you both."

"I refuse to listen to any more of this," Holly said. "It's completely out of the question. There's no way I'm going to marry him."

"I agree," said Skye. "I have no interest whatsoever in inheriting Tom's blasted estate."

"Oh, no?" Enraged now, Holly turned on him. "You tried to buy some of our land not long ago," she reminded him. "How do I know you and Grandpa didn't set this up between you? You want the land and you seem to want me, as well. This way you get both."

"Now wait just a minute. If you think I had anything to do with this, or that I knew about it in advance, you're dead wrong."

"Please, the two of you. I haven't finished," Geoffrey Bolton said. "If you don't agree to these conditions, which is to say, if you refuse to marry, the house—which, as I've stated, includes the barn and any additional outbuildings—and the land are to be sold to whichever real-estate developer is willing to pay the highest amount of money. There are several possibilities, I understand. Apparently Whittier, Montana, has the potential to become the next fashionable retreat from the city. Instead of fields, woods, mountains and grazing land, we'll have condos and dude ranches."

"I can't believe it. Grandpa would never have allowed that."

"If you decline to marry and the property is sold, you will not receive any of the proceeds from the sale, I'm sorry to say. The money is to be donated to—" Bolton paused and cleared his throat again "—the National Rifle Association."

"Oh, my God!" Holly cried.

This was too much for Skye. He sank down into a chair opposite the lawyer's desk, put his face into his laced fingers and howled.

Holly turned on him in outrage. "How can you laugh? Dammit, this isn't funny."

"Yes, it is," he said when he could speak. "It's hysterical."

"I'm not marrying you."

"Think of all the poor, helpless critters who'll die if you don't."

"That's the most ridiculous—"

"Hell, Tom was no fool. He knew which of us would be the more reluctant to go through with this preposterous scheme of his."

"Are you saying you're *willing* to marry me?"

He put his head to the side, considering. His eyes ran over her in a manner that humiliated her. "Marriage isn't exactly what I had in mind, but I guess I could live with it."

Her chin went up. "Well, I couldn't."

"Especially if it's only for six months," he amended.

"Kindly get that smirk off your face. This is serious. We made him a promise. A deathbed vow. I don't take something like that lightly."

Their eyes met and clashed. There was a pause; then Skye broke contact. He looked abashed. "Neither do I," he said in a more sober tone.

Geoffrey Bolton rose and headed for the door. "I'm going to excuse myself for a few minutes and allow you to discuss this matter in private."

"That's not necessary," Holly began, but the door was already closing behind him, leaving her alone with Skye Rawlins. It occurred to her that he seemed to have grown larger over the past few minutes. She hadn't realized he was quite so tall, or his shoulders quite so broad. She wished he weren't so damned attractive. She had a traitorous desire—demeaning under the circumstances—to put her fingers into that thick, dark hair of his and smooth it away from his handsome, rugged face. Angrily, she suppressed it.

"It's difficult for me to believe that you're not somehow responsible for this, Sheriff. How do I know you and my grandfather didn't cook this up together? You probably thought I'd go for it—marrying a stranger—because of what happened with Willy Hess. As if I need a man's protection—a *lawman's* protection—or some chauvinistic nonsense like that. Well, I don't. Hess is dead. And I don't need you or Grandpa or anybody else."

"Who's Willy Hess?"

Holly blinked. He sounded genuinely ignorant. She'd assumed her grandfather had told him what had happened to her.

"Does this have something to do with the vicious male Tom mentioned in his letter?" he asked when she didn't reply.

He was quick, she noted reluctantly. "I'm not going to discuss that with you." Reliving the assault and its aftermath was still very difficult for her. Besides, there was more to it than that. Much more. There were things she'd repressed, things she couldn't even remember.

"Anyway, that's not the problem," she said. "My grandfather's playing Cupid from beyond the grave is the problem."

"Look, Holly, I swear to you I didn't cook anything up with Tom. I'm as angry as you are. This is the first I've heard of his crazy scheme."

"He told me you wanted to get your hands on our land. After all, we've got pheasants, we've got ruffed grouse, we've got deer and elk and bear and maybe even some antelope. In the brooks and creeks that run through our property we've got rainbow trout. And browns. And cutthroats. Large-mouth bass in the lake. All sorts of fish, many of which I don't even know the names of. All living and feeding and propagating. All beautiful. All waiting for you to kill."

He released a long-suffering sigh. "I don't kill fish. I release them. If there were any way to catch and release a pheasant or a ruffed grouse, I'd do it. It's the joy of the hunt that I love, not the killing."

"Hunting's a blood sport. You can't deny the aggressiveness and violence at its core."

"I'd be glad to argue the matter with you on another occasion, but hunting is not the issue here."

"Yes, it is," she said, her lower lip trembling.

"Why?"

"Because I feel as if I'm the one being hunted. I know it's illogical, but that's the way I felt ever since you thundered out of the woods at midnight and carried me off on your stallion."

She's right, Skye thought. I wanted her then. I want her now.

Enough to marry her?

I must be as crazy as Tom, he thought, realizing he was considering it.

She's an herbalist. What the hell do you have in common?

I'm a hunter. We both love the wilderness.

She doesn't want you. Do you seriously think you're ever going to get to consummate this marriage?

Hell, I've charmed my way into the beds of a few reluctant women in my time.

She's vulnerable. You'll end up the way you usually do—hurting her and hating yourself.

Not this time. I promised Tom. I told him I'd take care of his granddaughter. I keep my promises.

Winning her *would* be a hunt, he concluded. Perhaps the most challenging one he'd ever undertaken.

It was irresistible.

Four

Holly was alone that night for the first time since her grandfather's death. Her herb students had stayed with her the first night, and several other close friends had flown in from Sedona for the funeral. They'd all left this morning, just before Holly had gone to Geoffrey Bolton's office, leaving her with tears, hugs, and many blessings and prayers, not to mention enough casseroles to last her a month.

She was sitting in front of a fire in the living room of Grandpa's rambling old house, once the main building of a struggling ranch. The rustic room resembled a hunting lodge, with its rough-finished woodwork and dusty old fixtures that gave off little light. There was a stag's head over the fireplace, a magnificent animal with a huge rack of antlers. There were ducks—both stuffed and wooden—on the top shelf of a bookcase. Several trophy-sized trout had been mounted on the walls.

In her normal state of consciousness, Holly found the place repellant, but tonight it didn't matter. She was weeping for her grandfather—silent tears continued to stream down her cheeks, an endless supply of them, it seemed—so his choice of decor did not seem important.

The rap on the door startled her. There were no close neighbors. "Who is it?" she called, quickly wiping her cheeks and eyes.

"Open up, Holly, it's me," drawled a voice that was becoming familiar. "Skye."

"What do you want?" She knew she must sound hostile, but what else could he possibly expect?

"We need to talk."

Reluctantly she unlocked the door. He was there on the threshold, all six foot two of him, clad in a blue denim jacket tossed carelessly over a black work shirt and a disreputable pair of jeans. He filled the narrow doorway with his broad shoulders and his uncompromisingly masculine air. His eyes were deep blue, fathomless and mysterious. His mouth was carnal, especially when tipped up in a smile.

Why not marry him? an imp inside her suggested. He's the closest thing to a hunk you've seen in a long time.

He entered, glanced around and said, "Have all your friends and assorted New-Age types left?"

"Yes." She led him into the darkened living room, where she was certain he would feel right at home. He'd probably shot one of those stuffed ducks himself. "Most of them have families to care for or shops to run. I'm going to have to get used to being alone."

He grinned. "Not necessarily."

"Don't start that again, please."

He sat down in an easy chair opposite the fire, stretching out his endlessly long legs. He was wearing scuffed Western boots, she noticed. He certainly wasn't her idea of a successful L.A. attorney. Why, she wondered, had he transformed himself into a Montana lawman?

"The way I figure it," he was saying, "we've got no choice. It's that wretched deathbed promise. He trapped us neatly, the clever old fox."

"This is the twentieth century. Almost the twenty-first. It's ludicrous to imagine being trapped into marriage."

"You'd be surprised. It still happens all over the world. There are still a lot of cultures where it's believed that young people are fools when it comes to choosing their mates. Much better that it be done by their older, wiser parents." He paused, then added, "The divorce rate in this country would tend to back that up."

"Well, you and I are not exactly young. And my grandfather was not always wise."

"No?"

"I adored him and I miss him terribly, but he was a romantic. Lord knows why he continued to believe in happy endings, given all the screwups in his life. In some ways, he was an overgrown child.''

''I think you underestimate him. He knew he was dying. He faced it and accepted it. I'd like to think I could be as brave, someday.''

What a typical male reaction, she thought. Their idea of character was all tied up with their ideals about the courage a man needs to face death. Didn't hunting have something to do with that ethic, as well? Ernest Hemingway and all that standing tall in the path of a charging rhino sort of stuff?

''It was life he didn't know how to face. He couldn't deal with the practical, the mundane. This house, this life, hunting, fishing…they represented an escape. He was hopeless at finances and miserable at relationships. He had no idea how to live in the real world.'' She knew she sounded testy, but she couldn't seem to help it. She was angry, she realized. Angry at Grandpa for dying!

''And you?'' asked Skye. ''Do you know how to live in the real world?''

''What's that supposed to mean?''

''I was curious. So I did some checking into the criminal history of a man named Willy Hess.''

She made a face. *Damn.*

''You want to tell me about it?''

''Sounds like you already know.''

''My information is somewhat spotty. I know he broke prison and came after you. It seems he violated quite a collection of laws—breaking and entering, assault and battery, assault with a deadly weapon, hostage-taking, unlawful restraint..." He paused. "I also know that he killed himself right before your eyes when the cops came and cornered him."

Holly folded her arms around her middle and shuddered.

"It must have been horrible," Skye said gently.

"It never should have happened. Willy was a violent man, a convicted felon. He should have been kept safely away from society where he wouldn't have been a danger to me or to anyone else. But he kept getting paroled and tossed back on the streets. It's really terrific—isn't it?—the way American justice works."

"The system's not perfect—"

"The system stinks! After a long history of vicious crimes, Willy Hess was finally imprisoned for life, without any hope of parole, but even that didn't stop him. Somehow he managed to escape and come after me. He made my life miserable for a very long time, and I can honestly say that neither the judicial system nor the Arizona police did much to protect me."

"Is that why you moved back to Montana?"

She sighed. "The real reason was Grandpa's cancer, but you're right, I didn't want to stay in Arizona. Even after Willy's death, I used to lie awake at night, hearing noises, and I couldn't walk down the street without continually glancing behind me. I felt hunted." She tilted her head to one side and appraised him. "Hess was a hunter, too. You even look a little like him.",

His eyes narrowed and the lines around his mouth deepened. "Give me a break, Holly. I'm one of the good guys."

The fire had died down. She moved to put another log upon it. It flared up immediately, casting tall shadows on the parlor walls. "I'm not so sure about that," she whispered into the hearth.

He came up behind her far too swiftly to anticipate. He touched her shoulders; she whirled around. She could see that he was angry. Perversely, she didn't care.

"Let go of me!"

His hands fell away. But he stayed intimidatingly close. "I heard that remark. I want an apology."

Wordlessly, she shook her head.

"Look, I understand that you're grieving and I understand that you're scared. But I've spent most of my career clearing the streets of slime like Willy Hess, and I won't be compared with him."

She bit her lower lip, feeling guilty. He was right. From the start, her response to him had been irrational and unfair. And what she'd just said to him had been downright rude.

"I've done my damnedest to help you out during the past few days, but you've received my efforts with no thanks and very little grace," he added. "What kind of way is that to behave?"

"You're right. I apologize," she said, feeling even worse. He'd helped with the funeral arrangements. He'd contacted friends of her grandfather whom she didn't know. He'd even brought food.

He was still angry. "I'm not responsible for Tom's idiosyncrasies. I feel as manipulated as you do. Do you seriously think I want a wife thrust upon me? I've successfully avoided marriage for thirty-six years."

She sneaked a look at him. He was frowning, his generous mouth thinned and hard. She liked the mustache. What would it feel like, she wondered, to kiss? *Don't think about it. You couldn't do it, even if you wanted to.* "Is avoiding marriage a goal of yours?" she asked.

She could have sworn the color came up in his cheeks. "No, of course not." He fidgeted for a moment with the band of his watch. "Well, maybe. At one time, I suppose it was."

"I've heard the gossip about you. Apparently you roll through women like an express train, leaving broken hearts and various other sorts of sexual and emotional wreckage in your wake."

His jaw tightened. "That's ridiculous."

"Is it?"

"I haven't even been dating lately. As for my past, if there have been a lot of women, it's because they're generally too smart to stick around for long. I'm no prize, believe me."

She waited, curious, but reluctant to press.

Skye ran a rough hand through his hair and paced back and forth a couple of times in front of the fire. "Look, the truth is, I guess I don't understand women very well. There's a certain solitary rhythm to my life, and I like it that way. I work hard, and my amusements—hunting and fishing—are not the sort of activities that appeal to the opposite sex. I'm independent, self-reliant. I tend not to let anybody too close, which is a protective thing, I suppose. Women can't stand that about me."

Holly was surprised. He seemed engaging and genial, and he was speaking now in a personal manner that would, she believed, appeal to most women. On the other hand, she reminded herself that they were only in the initial stages of getting to know each other. He was probably on his best behavior.

"It gets lonely sometimes," he went on. "Especially lately. There was someone, someone serious, someone I thought I loved, in California. But I waited too long, I guess, to consider commitment, marriage, family. Maybe if I'd brought it up a couple of years earlier, when *she'd* wanted it, but in the end she had a tough job in the D.A.'s office and no time to devote to children. Or to me."

He sounded bitter. It was crazy, she knew, but suddenly she wished she could make that bitterness go away. "So Grandpa was right? You do want—"

"I don't know what the hell I want," he said, stalking off toward the other side of the room.

Holly digested all this for several minutes. It was the first indication she'd seen of the shades and complexities to his character. Rather than alarm her, they made her like him more. He had conflicts inside him, like everybody else.

"How much did my grandfather borrow from you?"

Coming back toward her, he shook his head. "It's not important."

"To me, it is. I want to try to repay you."

"He's dead, and I consider the matter closed."

"How much, Skye?"

"Look, it doesn't matter. I can afford it. You can't. Let's forget it, okay?"

"The land he's left you must be worth several hundred thousand dollars. Surely he didn't borrow that much?"

Skye said nothing. But before he averted his eyes Holly read the silent confirmation there. My God, she thought, appalled.

"It was the cancer treatments," Skye said slowly. "He didn't have insurance. In some ways, you're right, he was unwise."

"He told me he had insurance!"

"He didn't want to worry you. Now that I know about the Hess affair, I understand why. Tom was extremely protective of you. He knew you had a lot on your mind."

Holly sat back down on the sofa. "He owed you a debt, and this is the only way he could think of to repay it." Unconsciously she took a pillow and hugged it to her middle. "I hate to admit it, but the will is fair."

"The will is insane. Probate is not my field, but I've got friends who are experts in that area. We'll break the damn will and that'll be the end of it."

"No." The look she turned upon him was fiercely determined. "We'll honor our promise to him. I owe a lot to my grandfather. I'll marry you, Skye. For six months. That's all we have to commit to. After that, we'll be free to split the property in a way that seems reasonable to both of us.''

He was leaning back against the near wall, his arms folded across his chest. She couldn't tell if he was pleased or dismayed.

"Maybe it won't be so bad," she added. "I suppose I can tolerate anything if I know it'll only last six months.'' She took a deep breath, hesitated, then blurted out, "I won't sleep with you, though. I'd like you to promise that you won't try to change my mind about that.''

Uh-uh, Skye thought. Dammit, that's not the way it's going to be.

Time to do a little dickering. Maybe she didn't feel anything for him, but since the moment he'd first seen her in Whittier, he'd been hot for her. At first it was pure chemistry, but now it seemed to be building into something with more potential. She might be prickly and independent, with crazy ideas about the evils of hunting and the sacredness of plants, but she was also an honorable woman who believed in paying her debts and keeping her promises. He liked her for that. Hell, he liked a lot of things about her.

She had a subtle vulnerability that touched his heart. The aloofness she'd exhibited so far made sense now that he'd understood what had happened with Willy Hess. Victims of violent crime learned not to trust people. It made them feel safer. Skye sensed that Holly yearned to feel safe.

Maybe I can't give her much, he thought, but I can give her that. Some other nut ever decides to come after her, he'll have to deal with me.

He pushed off the wall and moved to stand in front of her, conscious that remaining on his feet while she sat gave him a psychological advantage. "No more promises. If we wed, it'll be a real marriage. The will calls for a true union in every sense of the word."

"I don't think that means—"

"Yes, it does. It means we sleep together."

Flushing slightly, she said, "I'm not familiar with *your* personal habits, but *mine* do not include getting into bed with strangers."

"Neither do mine. What I propose is this. We marry as quickly as possible, to start the six months ticking. We live here together, as the will demands. The place is big, and we'll be able to give each other all the space we need. Separate bedrooms, at the start. We'll get to know each other." He smiled at her. "I'll court you."

She looked away and stared into the fire. She said nothing. At least, he thought wryly, she wasn't arguing.

"I'm not going to force myself upon you," he went on. "But I do want you, Holly. I won't deny it. I know you're grieving, and I respect that. You're probably not going to feel like opening up to anybody right now. I'm not going to hound you, but I will pursue you. Eventually, I hope, I'll wear you down."

She remained as still and silent as a fragile piece of sculpture. The firelight cast her shadow—surprisingly slim and supple—on the wall.

"Do you hear me?"

She turned her head. He was startled to see that her huge green eyes were awash with tears. "Yes, I hear you. What I hear is the voice of a hunter, anticipating the pleasures of the chase."

"Holly—"

"But what happens after you make the kill, Rawlins? What happens after you score? Six months is just about the right amount of time for a fling between two people who have so little in common. Any more than that and you'd be gone."

He forced himself to sound harder than he felt. "So what's the problem? A few minutes ago you were relishing the thought that you'd only have to tolerate me for six months."

Wordlessly, she shook her head. There's more to this, he realized. It was deeper, darker, more complicated.

"It's Hess again, isn't it?" He waited, but she didn't respond. "Holly, there was no mention of rape in the police report." He said it in a neutral tone, but knew she'd hear it as a question.

She was hugging herself. "If you're asking if that was what he intended, the answer is yes, unquestionably. And if you're also asking if it has affected my ability to have a normal relationship with a man, the answer is also yes. I haven't been with anybody since it happened. And I'm not sure that I want to be."

"Well," he said, embarrassed now, and ashamed of hassling her, "these things take time. I'm glad you told me. I know sometimes I come on a bit too strong." He stopped, reassessing rapidly. "But my proposal stands. We'll live together, but apart. We'll be patient with each other. Hell, I haven't been with anybody for a while, either. I'm, uh, used to it."

He thought he caught a hint of a smile. Encouraged, he went on, "Who knows what the coming months will bring? Maybe we'll drive each other crazy. Or maybe we'll get along. Maybe we'll even fall in love and all your fears will melt away. Live happily ever after and all that. Hey, don't look so skeptical. Anything's possible."

A definite smile turned up the corners of her mouth. She looked lovely when she smiled, he thought.

"I'm beginning to suspect that deep down inside you're as incurable a romantic as my grandfather was," she said.

"A hardheaded lawman like me? No way." But he could feel the tension in the room dispersing. He always knew when he'd convinced a judge, a jury. The opposition was about to fold.

"All I'm suggesting is that we keep our options open. No more crazy promises. We'll trust each other and see what develops. Maybe we'll be surprised."

She rose and faced him. "There are shadows inside me that I would love to be rid of. But if we get married, it's possible that my pain could somehow spread out and touch you. That's the last thing I want for you, Skye."

For some reason this touched him more than anything else she'd said. She sounded truly dismayed at the thought that she might be bringing her own problems down upon his head.

The impulse to take her into his arms and offer her shelter was almost too strong to resist. He did resist it, though. He didn't want her to think that he was making unwelcome advances.

"I'm willing to take that risk, Holly. And I'm willing to do my damnedest to make those shadows go away."

For an instant she looked so relieved that he thought she would be the one to embrace him. She was so close he could smell her—fresh, fragrant. Her skin was silk, her hair the color of a blackbird's wings. She stood there straight and tall, her shoulders squared, her gaze steady, but there was such a softness to her bottom lip, such vulnerability in the curve of her throat. He wanted to scoop her up into his arms and carry her upstairs, kicking down doors until he found a cozy bedroom. Lay her down and undress her. Soothe her fears and smother her dread. He could do it, he knew he could. The attraction between them was unmistakable, and the desire he felt for her was a hot but healing force.

"Okay," she said, and for one crazy moment he thought she was reading his mind. "I'll take the risk, too. I'll marry you, Sheriff. Let's go to Whittier tomorrow morning and start the process. You can move in as soon as it's done. I'll give you a nice room at the other end of the house."

He felt himself grinning like a schoolboy.

The hunt was on.

Five

As she contemplated her wedding, Holly felt a little like Persephone in the underworld. Skye Rawlins had swept down on her one night and carried her off on his black steed, and now she was honor bound to live with him for six months as the big sky closed over Montana, the plants withered in their fields, and the chill of autumn set in.

I'll be free, she reassured herself, at the end of March. With the coming of spring. As the wildflowers once again ventured to poke their heads through the thawing earth, she would be liberated from her bondage, independent once more.

The morning before the wedding—which would be ⁊ brief, impersonal ceremony in front of a justice of the peace—Skye moved in with a vengeance, bringing the first load over in a pickup truck. He was accompanied by a friend of his whom he introduced as Jake Cartwright, a tall, gold-haired man who, with his broad shoulders, slim hips and sulky mustache, was almost as sexy as Skye. There sure were some hunks lurking up here in the Montana highlands. She was missing Arizona less and less.

"Maybe you already know each other?" Skye asked. "Jake is the local sawbones around these parts. The man your granddad ought to have seen, if he'd had more sense."

Holly shook her head as Cartwright tipped his hat in the manner of polite wranglers everywhere. A physician, she thought weakly. Why did all these local professionals look as sexy as cowboys?

"Don't believe I've had the pleasure," he said. "Pleased to meet you, ma'am. I knew your grandfather. Liked him enormously. My condolences."

"Thanks. You've come to help Skye move his things?"

"Yup. It's my pickup. I have to admit, I never thought I'd see the day. Old Skye, roped and tied."

"You're not married yourself, Dr. Cartwright?"

"Nope. Skye and me, we're the last of the holdouts. We just can't seem to hang on to a woman for long. Shame."

What he really meant, she suspected, was that women had been unsuccessful at hanging on to *them*.

She looked in the back of the pickup truck, which was intricately loaded. "Lots of stuff," she commented.

"This is only the beginning of it," Skye told her as he and Jake began unloading a firm double bed, a worn but comfy-looking maroon leather recliner, several cartons of books and assorted odds and ends, and an expensive stereo-CD-tape deck combo with four enormous speakers.

But the biggest surprise was the frisky young golden retriever who leaped down from the cab of the truck.

"I didn't know you had a dog," Holly said, squatting to welcome the excited animal, who promptly slobbered all over her and offered her his paw.

"You like dogs, I hope."

"Love them. What's his name?"

"Barnaby. Barny for short. Uh-oh," he added as Holly continued to scratch Barny's ears and offer her face to be licked, "you're gonna spoil him, I can tell. Cut it out, Barny. Come!"

Holly laughed when the dog ignored him. "Well trained, I see."

"He's still young. Just over a year old. I've got to do some field training with him during the next few weeks. Toughen him up."

She stopped smiling. "You're training him to hunt?"

"Hell, Holly. He's a retriever. That's what he's for."

She offered to help them bring the rest of his things, but he and Jake refused. "Stuff's too heavy. You'll hurt yourself," Skye told her with typical masculine arrogance.

Fine, she thought. Her herbs needed tending.

The second load contained mostly office equipment, including file cabinets, an antique rolltop desk, several more contemporary office tables, a computer, printer, copy machine, two telephones and a fax machine. Sky and Jake Cartwright set all this up in what had been her grandfather's library.

"I got hooked on high tech in L.A.," he informed her. "Good way to keep track of nasty criminals."

The second load also contained Skye's personal items and clothes, including several spiffy-looking business suits. Holly knew that for the kind of office he'd worked in in California, he must have had to dress well, but jeans and leather seemed so well suited to him that she had trouble imagining him in anything else.

"How much more?" she asked as he departed again with the pickup.

"One more trip should do it, I think."

It was after the last trip that they had their first disagreement. He returned alone this time, now that the heavy items had been moved, and Holly watched in silence as he unloaded a ridiculous quantity of fishing equipment—fly rods and reels; fly-tying equipment, including several clear plastic bags full of feathers and furs from countless animals who had obviously been slaughtered for the purpose of luring trout with artificial insects; waders and vests and nets and all sorts of little gadgets whose purpose she could only guess at.

It looked as if he'd bought everything offered in the catalogue.

"You really need all this stuff to catch a bunch of stupid, unsuspecting fish?"

"Nah. I need it to catch the smart, wily ones." He grinned. "Actually, I don't use most of this junk. Anglers always have a lot of equipment they don't use. Just in case. You'd kick yourself if you lost a twenty-three-inch rainbow because you lacked a net to land him."

"It seems pretty unfair to the fish. All this arsenal of modern technology mounted against him."

"If that were true, trout would be easy to catch. Truth is, they're not. I'll take you fishing one of these days. Maybe down to the Big Horn. Then you'll see."

"No, thanks."

He began unloading several long, narrow objects in cases. At first she thought they were more fishing rods, but then she realized they were rifles. Or shotguns. Probably both.

Hands on hips, she blocked his entrance to the house. "You can take those back where you got them. I won't have any guns in my house."

"Hey, I'm the sheriff, remember?"

"And your only criminals around here are drunken teenagers and people who exceed the speed limit. You don't need this sort of arsenal for them."

"They're mostly for hunting," he admitted.

"That's what I figured. Please get rid of them."

"Sorry, but I'm not leaving firearms in an empty apartment. Someone might break in and steal them."

"I don't care, Skye. Lock them up in storage somewhere for six months."

"Well, darlin', problem is, this is the wrong six months. Fine if it were spring. But it's autumn. Hunting season's almost upon us, and I'm not giving up hunting, marriage or no marriage."

"If I can give up my freedom and my privacy, you can give up murdering birds and animals, for one season at least."

"Uh-uh, Holly, it's not negotiable. I'm a fisherman and a hunter. It's part of me, rooted in childhood. It's who I am."

"I won't have guns in my house," she repeated stubbornly.

"Then we got ourselves an impasse. What do we do, call off the wedding?"

"It's not a wedding," she snapped. "The word implies celebration, lots of friends and relatives, love and hope and joy. What it's going to be is a short, sterile ceremony in front of a justice of the peace. That's not my idea of a wedding."

His expression softened. "I'm sorry I can't give you the sort of celebration you deserve," he said slowly. "If it's any consolation, I feel cheated, too. This isn't happening the way I'd imagined it, either."

He was always sensitive to her feelings, Holly thought reluctantly. He might be a hunter, but he was also a kind man.

"Come to think of it, what we've really got here," he added with a wry glance down at the lethal object in his hands, "is a shotgun wedding."

In spite of herself, she began to laugh.

Skye immediately pressed his advantage. "Don't worry about the guns. They're always unloaded, and I'll store them out of your sight. But please keep this in mind—I know you're not happy with the American system of law enforcement. But I'll do a helluva lot better job defending the local populace from felons and thieves if I have access to my 'arsenal,' as you call it."

Ashamed of her own hypocrisy, Holly allowed him entrance.

Although he'd moved his belongings over, Skye did not ask to sleep there that night. After asking if she would mind watching his dog until the next morning, he went off to spend the evening before his wedding with Jake and some other friends. "One last chance to do a little serious male bonding," he told her with a grin.

Holly spent a solitary afternoon with her herbs— harvesting what remained from the growing season, which was nearing its end, bundling and hanging various herbs to dry and concocting a necessary tincture. Although her hands were busy, her heart was still grieving for Grandpa. She missed his company. She tried to tell herself that she ought to be cherishing her last chance to feel alone and independent, but since she knew herself to be basically a gregarious person who enjoyed the company of others, these thoughts did not provide much solace.

She passed the time on the evening before her wedding by playing with Barny—petting him, throwing balls and sticks for him, even grooming his thick golden coat with an old hairbrush. He was a large, sweet dog who communicated primarily by the changing expression in his large brown eyes. She quickly learned from looking into those eyes when he wanted to play, eat, sleep and go outside. She imagined she read a whole gamut of emotions there, and by the end of the evening she was laughing at herself. "I keep forgetting you're a dog, Barny. I'm treating you as if you were human."

Grinning sloppily, Barny thumped his tail.

Barny had an oval dog mattress with a red plaid cover that Skye had tossed on the floor of the bedroom at the far end of the hall where she had told him to put his personal things. When it was time to retire, Holly led Barny down to the room and showed him his bed. He sniffed it appreciatively and stepped onto it, circling three times before lying down and curling up. "Good boy. You have a nice sleep now."

With his head on his front paws, Barny watched as Holly pulled the shades and drew the curtains. But as soon as she shut off the light and left the room, he leaped up to follow her, his eyes surprised and injured now, as if to say, "Aren't you sleeping here, too? You're not going to leave me alone in a strange bedroom, are you?"

"I hope this doesn't presage the way your master's going to behave," she said as Skye's dog trotted confidently into her bedroom. He explored briefly, sniff-

ing everything, giving particular attention to the covers
on her bed, which must, she supposed, carry her scent.
"You're not sleeping here," she said in a tone that
tried—and failed miserably—to be severe. She liked
the company, she admitted to herself as Barny lay
down on the braided rug beside her bed and closed his
eyes.

She fell asleep, listening to the soft breathing of the
animal beside her. It was the first night since her
grandfather had died that Holly didn't feel bereft.

Six

"**B**y the authority vested in me by the state of Montana, I now pronounce you husband and wife."

Even though the words were uttered in the square confines of a dingy registry office instead of ringing out over the entire congregation in a church, they seemed momentous to Holly. It had happened. It was done. Standing beside her, his hands firmly clasping hers, was Skye Rawlins. Stranger. Hunter. Husband.

"You may kiss the bride," the justice added.

She'd forgotten that part. My God, she thought. We must be the only couple in the entire state who have never kissed until this moment.

She felt Skye shift and lean toward her. Cooperatively, she tilted her face up to meet his. Their first kiss was brief, polite and restrained. But as it ended, their eyes met, and she saw something he'd kept well hidden until now: an intense flare of passion and desire. To her surprise, deep inside her something tingled in response, and they both came alert for a moment, acknowledging it.

The wedding had seemed so cold-blooded—marrying because of a condition in a dead man's will. There were no real feelings involved, or so Holly had been trying to convince herself.

She'd been wrong. There were sexual feelings between them, and they weren't just his. I don't want this, she thought frantically. I just can't cope with it.

She wasn't aware that they were staring at each other, a silent duel of wills, until the justice of the peace cleared his throat. Skye backed off, grinning. He knows, she thought ruefully. Easy prey.

When they left the registry office shortly thereafter, exiting into the bright sunshine, Holly's emotions took another turn. "I was wishing Grandpa could have been here on my wedding day," she said as Skye helped her into his Jeep. He had another vehicle that he used for work, a huge-motored sheriff's patrol car, but there was no way, he'd told her, that he was going to show up for his wedding in that.

"I know. I'd have liked to have had some of my relatives here, as well."

She realized that she knew nothing about his family. Truly this was a man she didn't know. She'd married a stranger.

"Where are we going?" she asked as he put the engine into gear.

"Back to your place to change into something more comfortable. After that, a surprise."

"What sort of surprise? I really ought to work today, you know."

"No way, darlin'. This is our wedding day. It's a lovely September morning, and we're going to enjoy it. Winter comes early and hard in the high country of Montana. Are you game for an adventure?"

His voice was so vibrant and enthusiastic that she couldn't find it in her heart to go against him. "Sure, why not?"

His right hand moved from the gearshift to briefly squeeze her left one. It was gone before she could outwardly react, but inside her the afterglow from his kiss flared once more.

Skye took her riding. After they'd both changed into jeans and boots, he drove to the nearby stable where he kept Diablo and, after consulting with the wrangler in charge, secured a docile mount for Holly.

"This'll be an adventure, all right, since I don't know how to ride," she told him. "I know that's a little silly for someone born and bred in Montana, but my parents only took me once or twice when I was a child."

"Well, the one time I rode with you, you were a natural," he assured her. "Follow me over here into the corral, and I'll give you a brief lesson, then we'll head out onto the trail."

Holly quickly mastered the basics. With her spine straight, her heels down and her hands on the reins as loose and relaxed as she could make them, she and Misty, her dapple-gray mare, were slowly following Skye, Diablo and Barny up a narrow, pine-scented trail, into the hills that stretched away beyond the stable.

The countryside here was lovely—wooded hillside rising away in the distance toward the majesty of the Rocky Mountains. There was a rolling quality to the land all over Montana that was quite unlike anything Holly had experienced in other states. The vast blue sky seemed to hover more closely to the earth here than anywhere else she knew. It was a true melding of earth and sky and all the qualities that each contained.

The air was clean and fragrant with the scents of autumn, and the ground was freshly turned from harvesting. The trees were bursting into the color that would glorify their last few weeks in leaf before the starkness of winter set in. All around them as they rode, Holly could hear the sounds of small animals scurrying to stock their nests with enough food to last them through the long, harsh winter that loomed ahead.

The trail Skye had selected was an ascending one, which wound steadily through a woodland that seemed almost too thick to penetrate. "Watch out for some of these branches," Skye called back to her. He turned frequently to check on her progress, for which she was grateful. Barny ran back and forth between his

master and his new friend, wagging his tail furiously
and not seeming to mind that he was covering three
times as great a distance as everybody else.

Although Misty was proving to be a complacent and
responsive animal, Holly still didn't feel confident.
They were mostly walking, but every now and then
Diablo broke impatiently into a trot, which Misty
copied, and Holly found herself bouncing breath-
lessly in the saddle.

Grinning back at her on one of these occasions,
Skye said, "Off your rhythm?"

"I always seem to be bouncing *down* just as Misty's
rump is bouncing *up*."

"Trotting's probably the trickiest gait for the rider.
When we break out of the woods, we'll have some
clear, flat ground, and we'll do a little loping, which
is much more fun."

"If you're talking about going any faster than this,
Rawlins, count me out. I'm about to be bounced right
out of this saddle as it is."

He laughed. "Don't worry. I've never lost a stu-
dent yet."

Which made her wonder about his students . . . how
many of them were women. Because of his position
ahead of her, she could stare at him unobserved for as
long as she liked, a benefit of which she'd been taking
full advantage. Rangy and tall, with his craggy face
overshadowed by his broad-brimmed Western hat,
Skye Rawlins certainly cut a fine figure on horseback. He shed his jean jacket as the day grew warmer,
revealing a thin T-shirt that molded over the smooth

muscles in his shoulders. His spine was straight in the saddle, and the straddling position of his thighs pulled his jeans tight over hind-quarters that were, Holly decided, definitely worthy of appreciation.

"Can I ask you something?" she said, riding up beside him at a spot where the trail widened for several hundred yards. "Do you take all your girlfriends out on the trail? Is this a Montana man's version of dinner and a movie?"

"As a way to get her in the mood, you mean? Nah. Wouldn't work. You probably don't feel it yet, but an inexperienced rider like yourself is liable to end up sore in the most inconvenient places. I reckon that'll be a crimp in any devious plots I might have for seduction."

She giggled. "Actually, I can feel it already."

He grinned, but the look in his blue eyes remained serious. "You're bothered by this idea of me with a lot of girlfriends, aren't you?"

"Not really. It's no concern of mine."

"I'd say it is, given the circumstances. Hell, Holly, I'm thirty-six years old. There've been women, yeah, but no one lately. Nor is there likely to be. I'm married now."

She laughed uneasily. "Yeah. Tell me about it."

"We made some promises this morning. I know they're supposed to be temporary ones, but they had a final ring to them."

"Skye, this isn't a true marriage. Let's not begin harboring any illusions about that. True marriages are founded on love and commitment. We share neither of those."

He didn't reply. He had turned his head enough that the shadows thrown by the brim of his hat effectively hid his expression, and shortly thereafter, the trail narrowed again, forcing the two horses and the dog back into single file.

"We're near the top," Skye said. "Let's take a break. I brought some stuff for us to eat for lunch."

They had been climbing steadily for half an hour or so, zig-zagging up the steep side of a hill on a path that had grown increasingly narrow. Holly had been looking askance at the ground falling away behind them. If Misty were to make one false step... But fortunately, she seemed surefooted. Still, the prospect of clear, flat ground ahead was a relief.

Rounding a rocky crag, they broke out of the woods onto a high, spacious plateau. "Oh, Skye, how lovely," she said as he stopped and waited for Misty to move up alongside Diablo.

From the plateau they had a magnificent view of the surrounding countryside. Behind them stretched forest and scrub land, and ahead of them the mountains jutted up toward the heavens. The sun was at its zenith, its light brilliant and golden, and the air was clear and dry, with just the slightest edge that hinted of the coming fall. The plateau itself was a gigantic meadow, dotted with wildflowers. Delighted, Holly rode ahead to be among them, exclaiming over the robustness of the plants and the clarity of their colors.

"This is amazing. Look at the blue ones—those are cornflowers, and the white, of course, are daisies and Queen Anne's Lace. The bright yellow stars are Saint-John's-wort—a wonderfully healing herb—and the tiny golden sprays, of course, are the goldenrods. It's unusual to see them blooming together. It must have something to do with the elevation. Usually the goldenrod is the last to bloom, after the others have already wilted. This is a miracle to see them all ablaze simultaneously."

"They're beautiful," he agreed, dismounting. Barny began to bound around the field, stopping to relieve himself here and there, and sniffing the ground for game. "I know the daisies and the goldenrods, but I don't know much about the others. Hey, be careful," he added as Holly slid off Misty, stretched out her legs with a grimace, then bent over to jerk off her boots and socks. Barefoot, she walked into the field of flowers. "Aren't you afraid you'll cut or scrape the soles of your feet?"

"The soles of my feet are tough," she answered, tossing him a smile over her shoulder. "They're used to it."

"Well, uh, what about poison ivy?"

"It doesn't usually grow in open meadows."

"But it's plentiful in the woods around here, isn't it? Which reminds me, that night I came to find you in the forest, you were barefoot then, too. That looked like a prime spot for poison ivy to me."

"You're right—there used to be some there. It's gone now."

"What did you do? Nuke it with herbicide?"

She made a face. "Of course not. I'd never use any herbicide." She paused. "If I tell you, you won't believe me."

Skye followed her into the field of flowers. "Try me."

"Well, I explained to the plants that I needed the site for a sacred circle and asked them politely to move to some other location."

Skye blinked. He studied her expression for some sign that she was teasing him, but found none. "You asked them to move."

"Yes. Which they very kindly did. Next time I went back, the poison ivy was gone."

"Okay," he said doubtfully.

"Poor Skye." She was grinning. "Don't worry. Only six months to put up with this crazy woman, then you'll be free."

He frowned as if this statement didn't hold the appeal for him that it ought. "Just tell me this—do you speak English with these plants? What if I tried out my Spanish—would that work? Is poison ivy multilingual? Does it know Arabic or Japanese? Or did you have to learn some esoteric plant vocabulary before you could communicate?"

"Hey, I'm just telling you what happened. I don't speak in words—I try to sense the consciousness of the plant with my mind. Before I pick a plant, or gather its leaves or berries, I ask its permission."

"What if it says no?"

"Sometimes that happens. I get a sense of resistance, and I always respect that. I choose some other plant instead."

"Whoa. Twilight Zone."

"Do you remember, back in the early seventies, all that fuss about people who talked to their plants and made them grow faster? There was a book, *The Secret Life of Plants,* that documented some of the research. There were experiments suggesting that plants have some kind of consciousness, that they react when in the presence of strong emotion. When something near them dies, for instance, they seem to know it, as if they sense a disruption in the force field around them."

"May the Force be with you." He smirked.

She ignored him. "In one famous experiment, two plants were placed side by side in a lab while six human volunteers filed through the room. One of them, chosen at random, grabbed one of the plants, uprooted it, and ripped it to shreds. The electromagnetic sensors on the second plant went wild as it witnessed this event. It was scared."

"Can't say I blame it," Skye said dryly.

"A few hours later the six volunteers were once again ordered to walk through the room. The surviving plant showed no response to the five innocent humans, but when the murderer entered the room, its sensors careened off the chart. Not only did the plant remember the crime, it recognized the perpetrator."

"You're kidding me."

"It's God's truth. Read the book."

"Jeez, instead of deputies, maybe I should get myself a couple of rosebushes. 'Course, they wouldn't be much help on a stakeout, and I don't know how we'd question them on the witness stand, but, hell, it's not right to let all that talent go to waste. Cactus Harry, Detective First Class, Homicide."

She laughed. "I told you you wouldn't believe me."

"You were right. Next time, I'd better not ask." He brushed the palm of his hand over a stalk of goldenrod that thrust up between them. "So you really make medicine out of some of these plants?"

"Yes, of course." Skye, she noted, had been gradually moving closer to her during this discussion. He was at her side now, their shoulders nearly touching.

"Throughout history, people have always made medicine from plants," she said, forcing herself to concentrate. "They still do. Some of the most powerful drugs known come from plants—heart-rhythm regulators, painkillers, even cancer-fighting agents."

"Yeah?" There was a slight smile on his mouth—it tipped his mustache up in an angle that she found enormously appealing—and she suspected that he was more skeptical than he would admit of herbal medicine. This didn't faze her. Holly loved what she could do with herbs, but she didn't consider herself to be a fanatic on the subject.

"You don't believe me, do you?" A low tangle of weeds caught her foot and she stumbled. Skye's hand shot out, gripping her upper arm. "Thanks," she said, righting herself. Both of his hands slid to her waist now, steadying her. His fingers were full of sunlight. Warm.

"What don't I believe?" He turned her around to face him. He was very close.

"Uh, the healing power of herbs." Holly could feel the wildflowers tickling her bare feet, legs and knees.

"I'm kind of a rationalist," he said slowly. "This is the way I figure it—if herbal medicine has always been around and always been so effective, then how come it wasn't until the advent of modern medicine—surgery and antibiotics—that people's life spans increased by thirty or forty years?"

"I don't deny the miracles of modern medicine. Herbs work best when they're used slowly, over a long period of time. There are some urgent medical conditions that can't be treated that way. But there are many others that can."

One of his fingers worked its way up her side to her shoulder, where it wound itself through an errant lock of her hair. "Working slowly has its appeal, but there's something to be said for urgency, as well."

She knew it was going to happen before it did. She told herself she should try to stop it. But she didn't want to stop it . . . and then it was too late.

His arms slid around her, gently but rough, imprisoning her. It was not a tentative embrace, nor the brief, slightly embarrassed kiss they had shared in front of the justice of the peace. This time his kiss was full and deep and long.

His lips took hers with demanding masculine authority, parting them, nipping them lightly. Then his tongue penetrated, shocking her with the intensity and the intimacy of his invasion.

Holly made a small sound in the back of her throat as she avidly returned his kisses. She could feel the soft hairs of his mustache against her upper lip and, as he moved her closer, the outline of his hard-muscled body through his denim jeans. Her own clothing seemed paper-thin as one of his arms tightened around her waist and the other hand cradled the nape of her neck, slipping beneath the long fall of her thick black hair to caress her bare skin. She squirmed, startled by her intense desire to feel his naked flesh against her own. There was heat between them, fire. The whole world seemed to be tilting on its axis, but it was only her spine arching as he pulled her closer, tongued her deeper.

And then, just as suddenly as he'd started, he stopped. He lifted his head and raised his palms to her face, cupping her cheeks. "You scared?" he asked, his voice husky, gentle.

Confused, she shook her head. She felt no fear; she felt dizzy... and alive. Her body's response had been instant and powerful. Must be pheromones or something, she thought wryly. One of those chemical reactions that the world is so quick to call romantic love. Or maybe it was simply deprivation. It had been a long, long time since there had been a lover in her life.

"I don't want you to think I'm pressing the issue, or attempting to rewrite the rules," he said. "I just want you to know that you needn't be afraid of me or of what I feel for you."

"Okay," she said shakily. She was embarrassed to note that her fingers had been clinging to his shoulders for several moments longer than was strictly necessary. Moving away, she tipped her head back to find that he was grinning at her, looking simultaneously boyish and seductive. Devil, she thought. Even so, she found herself smiling back. She was here with a handsome man in a miraculous place where wildflowers knew no season, and she felt absurdly happy.

"Hey, I've got an idea."

"I'll bet you do." She could hear the teasing lilt in her own voice. Goodness, she thought. Listen to me. I'm flirting with him.

"We could just sorta stretch out among all these beautiful flowers and inhale their fragrance and each other's and feel their texture and each other's and—"

"Please don't push it, Skye," she said, warning herself as much as him.

His knuckles lightly brushed her cheek. "Okay. I won't."

"I don't even know you yet."

"Well, hell, woman. That's the point. You get to know me, you might not like me." He spoke lightly, but there was a flash in his eyes that told her that at some level, he meant exactly what he said.

He was still too close. Here they were together in a perfect place on a lovely day, two strangers who were husband and wife. She retreated another couple of steps just as Barny began excitedly barking.

Skye turned away, looking toward the spot where his dog was wildly wagging his tail and running back and forth in front of a thicket of brambles, intent on something only he could see.

"Hush, boy," Skye called to him. "Stop your noise."

Barny obediently stopped barking, but seemed ready to plunge into the brambles.

"What's he doing?"

"He's making game. Means he's into an animal or a bird—a grouse, probably, given the high terrain— that he's about to flush. He's doing his job pretty well, too, for a beginner."

They watched as Barny shot forward into the thicket. There was a crack of wings as the bird, which was indeed a grouse, rose into the air and flew off toward the east.

"Good dog," Skye called after him when Barny extricated himself from the brambles. "Come. That's a boy. Good dog. Sorry there's nothing for you to retrieve. But you'll make a crackerjack partner in time."

Fists on hips, Holly glared at the two of them—Skye praising his dog for flushing the bird and Barny wagging his tail proudly. "If this had been grouse-hunting season and you'd had your shotgun, you'd have killed that bird, right?"

He shrugged. "I'd have tried. Missed, probably. I miss a lot."

"I can't understand how you can justify killing innocent birds and animals."

"I stopped trying to justify it a long time ago. People who hunt understand. People who don't—well, they've got their own passions. Everybody's got something they learned to do, in childhood maybe, or at some critical point in their lives, that makes them feel happy and serene and whole. I don't begrudge others their vital recreations, and I don't expect them to begrudge me mine."

Somewhat chastened, she said, "Did you learn to hunt in childhood?"

"Yup. With my father and my grandfather. They taught me a lot of important things, among them an abiding love and respect for the whole spectrum of nature, with all its beauties and its cruelties."

"I see the cruelty in hunting, certainly, but none of the beauty."

"That's because you're a modern woman in a modern society that can afford to hire strangers to slaughter meat, fish and fowl. And other strangers to wrap it in pristine little packages for you to pick up at the grocery store."

"You live in the same modern society, Skye. Because that grocery store exists, you don't need to kill to eat."

"Any more than you need to uproot and murder plants to make the herbal remedies that treat the same illnesses that the big pharmaceutical companies can knock out with synthetic chemicals?"

She opened her mouth to protest, but ended up grinning instead. "Touché."

He smiled, as well, then whistled for the horses and began unpacking the saddlebags. He brought out bread, cheese, fruit and a bottle of wine. "Speaking of groceries, how about some lunch?"

* * *

Both Holly and Skye were quiet that evening on the way home, a comfortable silence at first that grew somewhat more tense as he turned into the long drive that led to the ranch. Night had fallen in the swift, surprising way it does in the fall. Darkness cloaked his face, and on her own was a gloom relieved only by the tiny green and amber lights winking on the Jeep's dashboard. She glanced over at him, thinking once again, This man is my husband. As in "forsaking all others, as long as you both shall live."

He was intent on his driving, his gaze forward, his gloved hands firm on the steering wheel except when his right hand moved skillfully between their bodies to manipulate the gearshift. Once, by accident, his knuckles on the stick had brushed her thigh, but the contact had been fleeting, unacknowledged. She had felt it, though. The brief invasion of her personal space, innocuous though it had been, electrified her.

They had ridden for most of the day, and Holly's limbs were aching. Yet, exhausted though she was, she felt excited, too. Intoxicated. There was something heady about spending time with Sheriff Skye Rawlins. Stranger. Hunter. Husband.

When he stopped the Jeep in front of what had been her grandfather's house, flipped open the back door to let Barny out, then glanced over at her, Holly crossed her arms over her lap in a self-protective gesture. This was their wedding night. And, during the course of the day, something had changed between them. A certain intimacy had been created during the hours together. A sense of ease with one another. And something else, something that was rising up now, with the coming of darkness, and seeking further expression.

Meeting his eyes, she could see the faintly quizzical look on his face—his eyebrows arched, his lips, that sexy mouth angled up in a cautious smile. Her body thrilled to the memory of that mouth on hers...those strong arms around her. It had been lovely, that brief passion in the sea of wildflowers.

From the way he was looking at her, she sensed that he was asking her permission to explore that passion a little more tonight. And her strongest impulse was to smile and nod and grant it.

No, she ordered herself. A kiss was one thing. But anything more . . . that way darkness lies.

"Holly? What are you thinking?"

Unhooking her seat belt, she tossed him a half smile. "Nothing. I'm just tired. It's been a long day. Lovely, though. Thank you."

"My pleasure," he drawled.

He was out his side and around to hers before she could extricate herself. The old-fashioned gesture of holding the door for her touched her. A cowboy and a gentleman.

Together they climbed the four steps that led to the front porch. Outside the door to the house, she fumbled in her pocketbook for her keys. "We'll have to have a set made for you," she said as she found the correct one, inserted it into the lock and twisted. As she pulled it out, the key ring slipped from her fingers and fell to the porch. She and Skye bumped heads as they simultaneously stooped to retrieve it.

"You're nervous, aren't you?"

"Who me?" she said, giving him a crooked smile. She moved to enter the house, but his hand on her shoulder prevented her.

"Wait," Skye said. "We're man and wife. Let's do this properly."

Before she could anticipate his action, he bent and slipped one arm under her knees and lifted her into his arms. She automatically reached an arm around his neck, which brought his head down close to her face. His dark mustache was nearly touching her. She could feel his breath upon her lips.

She laughed as he carried her across the threshold. Barny followed them in, eyeing them curiously.

"Put me down, Skye. You'll hurt yourself."

"As a matter of fact, you're a damn sight heavier than you look," he teased her, but he kept carrying her until they were well within the house, kneeing the excited Barny out of his way and finally setting her down near the foot of the staircase that went up to the bedrooms.

He stretched and arched his back to loosen it, then reached down to stroke the dog. "Ow. That'll teach me to make romantic gestures."

"It was a very nice gesture," she heard herself say. "Particularly," she added, backing away from the heat in his electric blue eyes, "if you're anywhere near as stiff and sore as I am. I loved the riding, but I probably won't be able to walk tomorrow. Or sit."

"A hot bath is just the thing for that. But what you really need is a good rubdown. May I offer my services? I give a pretty good therapeutic massage."

"Uh, no, thanks. I'm really tired. I think I'll just go up and fall into bed."

"Holly—" He was reaching for her, moving into an embrace, about to take her and kiss her and caress her and break her down...

"No, Skye," she whispered.

Groaning, he ran a shaky hand through his hair. "Holly, you're so sweet, so passionate. I want to be with you. I've wanted it since the moment we met."

But she was shaking her head, backing away. "Skye, I can't. Not yet. I'm really sorry, but I just can't. Good night."

Turning, she fled up the stairs, leaving Skye at the bottom sadly shaking his head. Well, hell, he thought. The chemistry was there between them. Her warm response to his kiss in the meadow had left no doubt about that. She knew he wanted her. And for all her skittishness and evasiveness, he strongly suspected his desire was returned.

They were married; this was their wedding night. For the first time in his life, he had a legal right to be with a woman. He was tempted to follow her upstairs and press the issue a bit.

But how could he? Holly was afraid of something, something he didn't entirely understand. He'd promised to be patient with her. She'd made it clear when she'd agreed to this marriage that she expected his patience to hold.

Sitting down on one of the bottom steps, he made a fuss over Barny, patting and playing with him, throwing a soggy tennis ball that he delightedly retrieved. "She's no fool, is she, boy? Smart lady, refusing to get mixed up with me."

Barny grinned and wagged his tail, his intelligent brown eyes focused on the ball in his master's hand.

"A kinder, more honorable man would back off and leave her alone, but I'm not going to do that, am I? Sit, boy."

Barny sat. *Thump, thump, thump* went his tail on the hardwood floor.

"Not me, not old Skye. I know there's something in her past, something awful, but I'm not going to let that stop me, am I? Uh-uh. I'm going to take it upon myself to cure her—the hero to the rescue." He shook his head in disgust.

Barny whined for him to throw the ball.

"I'll be patient, yeah, but ultimately I'm going to chase her down, flush her out, take careful aim and fire off my best shot. Chances are, sooner or later, I'll bring her down. Nice guy, huh? What the hell am I trying to prove?"

Skye heaved the ball, low, into the living room. "Good dog," he said as Barny tore after it. "I sure wish my life were as simple as yours."

Seven

"**I**'m afraid I've got a bit of a problem," Skye said
to Holly one Saturday morning over the breakfast table. He was eating a huge plate of ham and eggs, the
very smell of which was distasteful to Holly, who stuck
mostly to a vegetarian menu. Her breakfast consisted
of Swiss muesli cereal, fresh fruit, tea and a little plain
yogurt. "There's something going on in town that we
need to discuss."

"I'm listening," Holly said, sipping her Lapsang
souchong tea and thinking how handsome, if scruffy,
Skye looked early in the morning. He hadn't shaved
yet, and the rough, shadowy growth of his whiskers
was erotically appealing.

"I've been getting some complaints. As sheriff, I mean. There's one old mischief-maker, Roy Galleger is his name, who's always sticking his nose into other folks' business. He's got himself some friends, also the nosy type, and together they've been stirring up trouble."

"What sort of trouble?" Holly asked. They'd been living together for more than a month now, and she was getting used to listening to him talk about his work. She liked it, in fact. He seemed to be as much a social worker as a law enforcer here in this small town—interceding in domestic disputes, helping drunks get off the sauce, finding and counseling runaway teenagers. It was much more rewarding than the high-paying litigation he'd been doing in L.A., he'd told her, which was exactly what he had hoped when he'd returned to Montana.

"Trouble concerning you, I'm afraid."

"Me. What on earth do you mean?"

"Well, it seems there are some wild rumors flying about you and your out-of-town women friends. Midnight meetings in the woods, strange songs and chantings, mysterious drugs and potions, not to mention strangers coming into Whittier for a weekend then disappearing without doing business at any of the local stores. Galleger's going so far as to whisper that the sheriff's new wife is a witch who's put a spell on him."

Holly laughed. She couldn't help it.

"Yeah, I know. I've been ignoring these idiots for weeks, but I'm beginning to get concerned," Skye said. "Galleger's calling for an investigation. If the local law won't handle it, he's all for calling in the state boys, which is the last thing I need.''

''There's nothing strange or mysterious about herbal medicine. It's as ancient as humanity itself. No one ever gossiped or raised community concerns about us in Sedona.''

''That's because Sedona, Arizona, scenic though it is, is one helluva strange town. They've got all those vortex nuts there, not to mention folks walking around who claim to have just stepped off a flying saucer. This is hardheaded, no-nonsense Montana. Here in Whittier, someone like you is considered, uh, eccentric.''

''Do you consider me eccentric?''

He pushed back his chair and tipped it onto its rear legs. ''Truth is, I don't know what to think. You've got some weird friends coming to town for your seminars, and when you go out to do your moon circles, or whatever they are, in the woods at night, I'll admit it all seems pretty strange to me.''

''Now there's a vote of confidence. Tell me, Skye, do you believe I've put a spell on you?''

He grinned outrageously. ''I reckon there's no doubt about that. I've been under your spell since the day we met.''

She smiled briefly, but what he was telling her was disturbing. It hadn't occurred to her that anybody in Whittier might be gossiping. ''This is so typical of what has always happened to women. Get a group of us together for any purpose, and you men get nervous. Before long you're calling us witches and attributing all manner of mischief and mayhem to us.''

"Don't work yourself into a feminist rage. I happen to be on your side."

"Doesn't sound like it."

"I was just trying to help you see yourself and your friends the way an outsider might see you. Most folks go to square dances or church suppers on Saturday nights, but you go out in the woods and chant around a fire. That makes some people uneasy. At heart, I think a lot of modern Americans—males *and* females—are superstitious. They fear anything they don't understand."

She sighed. "So what can I do about it?"

"Well, you could stop being so secretive, for one thing. Maybe let somebody observe one of your circles—not participate, mind you, but just be there, quietly, keeping his eyes open and his mouth shut. That somebody could then report back to the townspeople that nothing untoward goes on at one of these meetings, that it's all a lot of harmless nonsense. Then, I think, some of the gossip would die down."

She raised her eyebrows. "You're inviting yourself? As my husband, you're not exactly an objective witness."

"No, but I'm trusted in Whittier. And I'm the sheriff."

"We don't typically include men. It's a women's ceremony."

"What do you do, take off all your clothes and dance around naked?"

Holly smiled. "Now there's a male fantasy. If we did that, I'll bet every man in Whittier would be sneaking into the woods to try and catch a glimpse."

"I know I would."

"Seriously, Skye, you already know what we do. You were at one of my circles on the night my grandfather died."

"That was only for a couple minutes. I didn't see the whole thing. Besides, I thought you did it differently each time."

"A little bit differently," she admitted. "Depending on the group."

"You doing one tonight?"

"I'd been planning to, but several of my friends called to say they couldn't make it this weekend, so I canceled it. I was thinking of having my own private ceremony, though. The moon is full tonight. But I don't suppose you'd be interested in that."

"I'm interested in anything you're interested in. Count me in."

She was touched by the warmth and sincerity in his voice. It was impossible to doubt that he meant exactly what he said.

During the weeks since their wedding, Holly and Skye had been coexisting peaceably, their separate routines meshing with each other. Their conflicts had been surprisingly few. Long accustomed to making a home for himself, Skye did not expect any sex-linked divisions of household labor. Since he knew how to cook, shop, vacuum, do dishes and laundry and scour a toilet bowl, they quickly fell into a pattern of sharing such chores. If anything, he was neater and better organized than Holly, although not obsessively so.

They both spent long hours over their work, which kept them apart during the day, and sometimes, when Skye changed shifts with one of his deputies, during the nights, as well. Holly always had something to do—either teaching and entertaining the students who came up on the weekends for her seminars, grading the work of her correspondence school students, or preparing and bottling her herbal extracts for sale by mail order.

On the evenings when they were both home, they gently mocked each other's choice of leisure activity. Holly had a couple of TV dramas that she hated to miss, and Skye was hooked on just about every variety of professional sports. There was a pitched battle one evening when the World Series conflicted with *L.A. Law*.

Usually, though, Holly was glad when the game in question went on late, since this made it easier for her to escape to her bedroom without attracting Skye's attention. The only time she really felt uncomfortable with him was at night, when the darkness settling around the isolated house closed them in together and created an intimacy that neither one of them really wanted to ignore.

Yet they did ignore it. Since the night of their wedding when she had left him at the bottom of the stairs, they had not touched, except in the most accidental of circumstances. No kisses, no embraces. They were careful never to invade each other's personal space, so careful that it was painful at times.

Rather than ease, this cautiousness tended to increase the physical tension between them. Holly was always conscious of him—where he was in the room, how far away, how near. The more she tried to avoid his body, the more she yearned to run into his arms. The more she tried to convince herself that any love-making between them would be the source of nothing but fear and heartache, the more she longed to invite him to her bed.

But she did not invite. And he did not entreat. Their marriage remained a union in name only.

It couldn't continue. Both of them, she sensed, were reaching the limits of their patience and endurance.

"So how about it? May I come this evening?" he asked her.

"If you come," she said slowly, "you can't just watch. You have to participate."

"Uh, what exactly does that mean?"

"I'm afraid you'll just have to wait and see."

"Okay. I'm game."

"But if you do anything to criticize, make fun of, or disrupt what I'm doing—"

"I won't. I promise. I'll behave myself."

"You'd better, Sheriff, or I *will* put a spell on you."

Maybe this wasn't such a hot idea, after all. Skye was watching his lovely wife prepare the sacred fire deep in the forest that evening. He felt uncomfortable. Out of his element. Vulnerable. There was noth-

ing he wanted more than to go back to the house, turn
on the television, and lose himself in a nice, normal
game of football. He wasn't into this weird, spiritual
stuff. Good thing old man Galleger wasn't here, he
was thinking. He'd freak.

Prior to coming outside, she'd behaved no differently, in his opinion, from a Girl Scout getting ready
for a night in the woods. With his help she'd assem-
bled a few necessities, like firewood, matches and in-
sect repellent. She'd given them to him to carry, while
she prepared a basket filled with crystals, wands, can-
dles, herbs and goodness only knew what other mystical items.

But on the way out to the site in the woods Holly
had chosen for the ceremonial fire, her mood had altered. She had begun to seem very different from the
Holly MacLeish whom he believed he knew so well. As
they walked—she determinedly barefoot—toward the
site where she held her circles, she asked him to maintain silence.

"Listen to the murmurings of the earth, our
mother," she'd said in her lovely, low contralto.
"Look up and see the moon and stars scattered across
the firmament. Listen for the music of the spheres."

Mesmerized by her beauty, which seemed more radiant than ever tonight, with her long black hair loose
and freely blowing in the breeze and her skirt a blaze
of color that even the darkness could scarcely dim,
Skye looked and listened and believed he heard. There
was magic in the night, and Holly was part of it. The

forest was her natural element, and he, who had lived here for most of his life, felt like an intruder.

At the site near the spring where Skye had invaded her circle once before, Holly stopped to make her fire within a ring of large stones that had obviously been placed there for the purpose. She treated the fire-making as a sacred act, building it slowly and ritualistically, invoking the powers of the four directions, east, north, south and west, in what Skye believed to be a tribute to Native American beliefs.

"Is this some sort of religious thing?" he had asked her that evening while they were gathering the firewood. "Are you and your friends pagans or something, worshipping the gods in rocks and brooks and trees?"

"I go to church, Skye, you know that," she had answered, and indeed, she did attend the local Sunday services a lot more often than he did. "But I believe you can find God in many ways, in many places. In the natural world, especially. I guess I wouldn't call what we do religious in the conventional meaning of the word, but it is sacred, if that makes any sense to you."

It did. He had often found sacredness himself, in the forest. For him, hunting was a mystical experience, a time to feel an ancient drawing back to his roots as a male. He had never been able to explain to Holly how it felt to enter the woods as a predator, no different from the hundreds of other predators of every species who hunted there daily to subsist. How he became part of the world he entered, how he watched and listened and used his instincts, how he imaginatively became one with his prey. She wouldn't understand it, he'd thought. Only when you entered the land to hunt, as all animals hunt, could you truly know what it was to live upon the land, in the land, with the land.

Watching her now, though, he realized that she, of all the women he had ever known, could best understand what it was to be an outdoorsman. How it felt, what it meant. It was too bad, really, that she had such a passionate aversion to hunting, because he and Holly were a lot more alike than either of them had thought.

"Now what?" he asked when the fire was well established.

"Stand right there, opposite me."

He faced her across the fire and watched in silence while she took up a wand with a thick knob at one end that was covered with red cotton. As she touched it to the flames, he realized it was a torch. The end must be filled with herbs, since it released a fragrant odor as it burned.

Holding the torch aloft, Holly took several steps back. Stretching out her arm, she began to walk sunwise, from east to west, clockwise around the circle, inscribing a larger circle in the air with the flames from the torch.

"What are you doing?" he whispered. He felt slightly in awe of her. With her long hair flowing down over her back and shoulders, its black sheen reflecting the light from the fire and the torch, she looked otherworldly. He was reminded of ancient tales of mortal men who dared to fall in love with goddesses . . . and the tragedy that was the inevitable result.

"Casting the circle," she answered, which increased his awe. It was a witchy thing, surely, casting a circle. As she came around behind him, closing him into the circle of light, he felt for a moment like bolting. This was not the same Holly MacLeish whom he admired every morning over the breakfast table. That Holly was warm, gentle, adorable. This woman, with her intensity and dedication, her authority and her passion, scared him a little. He wasn't sure what to make of her.

She had returned to her original place opposite him, closing the circle with a sweeping gesture in the air. With her eyes closed and her face composed, she intoned, "Peace to all the members of this circle. We lift up our hearts and place them within, here in this protected space, safe from all harm. Blessed be."

Was he supposed to "amen" that? he wondered. Uncertain, he kept his mouth shut.

"Do as I do," Holly said, "and repeat after me."

"Sure. No problem."

After planting the torch just within the ring of the fire, she raised her arms high over her head. Self-consciously, Skye did the same. He found himself staring at her breasts through the diaphanous fabric of her Gypsy blouse. He could clearly see the straps of her bra. It looked feminine and fragile—pretty underwear, not the plain, utilitarian kind.

"Aspire toward the light," Holly said. Her forest-green eyes were closed and her hands were reaching toward something overhead he could not sense or see.

"Aspire toward the light," he repeated, feeling ridiculous.

She dropped her arm to shoulder level and cupped her palms. "Receive the light." As he watched, her expression altered. The yearning was replaced with a look of wonder, pleasure and joy. "Receive the light," he said, wondering what it was that she was experiencing.

Moving slowly, she crossed her arms at breast level and he copied her, feeling the steady beat of his heart as he hugged himself. "Incorporate the light." Her face was intense, as if she were actively doing something, and beneath her eyelids, he noticed that her eyes were jumping about, the sign of dreaming or visualization.

"Incorporate the light," he repeated.

Her hands moved in semicircles around her, palms outward. "Radiate the light," she said, and he blinked, for it seemed to him that she *was* radiating light. Her face was aglow, and he could swear that as her hands moved, light moved, also. It's just the firelight reflecting from her rings and bracelets, he told himself, but he felt spooked, anyway.

"Radiate the light."

"Aspire toward the light." Once again, she raised her arms heavenward. Skye repeated it, closing his eyes this time. He tried, mentally and physically, to aspire. Maybe he wasn't the aspiring type.

"Receive the light."

Did he feel something? Hmm, maybe so. A voice in the back of his mind seemed to be saying, "The light is all around you, always, everywhere. All you need do is open yourself to it. Open yourself and receive."

This time when she said, "Incorporate the light," Skye envisioned warm white light flowing through him from head to toe. It moved down his legs, out along his arms, into the tips of his fingers. Amazingly, he felt himself relaxing, getting into it. He felt warm, peaceful, content.

"Radiate the light," she intoned, and as he put his palms out to do it in the manner she'd shown him, his hands accidently brushed hers. His eyelids popped open, as, for an instant, did hers.

She cleared her throat. "Aspire toward the light," she said firmly, but Skye lost any transcendental feelings entirely as desire flooded through him. Standing there, so tall and slender, so beautiful, so earnest, so powerful in her womanhood, Holly MacLeish was so much the woman he wanted. I'm aspiring, all right, he thought, dropping his arms, but it's toward darkness. Toward a warm, midnight place in which to take her, undress her, arouse her, invade her. Penetrate that feminine mystery in the manner of men from time immemorial. Capture all that loveliness and energy and hold it for my own.

"Holly," he said, interrupting her litany.

She didn't answer.

"Holly," he repeated, moving toward her.

She must have sensed it because her hands came up, off schedule, palms outward—radiating light to him? Or warding him off? The latter, he fancied.

Then she opened her eyes and reached into the leather pouch she carried at her waist. Into his outstretched hands she placed a mound of strong-smelling herbs. "There is more," she told him, as if to restrain any idea he might have about disrupting the ceremony. "At this point you must release to the fire something that is holding you back in life."

Damn, he thought. "What if I don't wish to be rid of anything?"

"I've never met anybody with that particular difficulty before," she said with a smile.

"I'm not sure what you mean," he said. "You go first."

Nodding, she took a handful of the herbs, approached the fire and added a log to it. "Blessed be," she said again.

"You always say that. What's it mean? Is it like amen?"

"Yes. It's also a greeting, a valediction and a prayer of thanks. It's the acknowledgment of the bounty of the universe and the blessedness of all things."

"Oh. Well, blessed be," he said awkwardly.

She smiled at him, then, cupping her herbs in one hand, she closed her eyes and knelt in the dirt. She appeared to be meditating. She drew a deep breath and blew it out, gently, into the herbs in her palm.

"I release to the fire my darkness and shadows," she said in a barely audible voice. "And my fear of confronting the events in my past." She opened her hands and let the herbs fall into the fire, where they let off a heady fragrance as they were consumed.

Hmm, thought Skye. Interesting prayer. How long would it take for it to work?

Rising and stepping back, she gestured to him to approach the fire. He did so, not knowing what he was going to say until he heard himself speaking the words. "I release to the fire the hesitancy that has kept me from acting to seize the things, and the people, who could bring happiness into my life."

When he tossed the handful of herbs she had given him, the tiny particles sparkled in the flames, radiant for an instant, beautiful, as if some power that resided therein had heard his wish and decided to grant it. Then he looked up and saw that Holly was watching him, that she had heard his words, and that she was, very faintly, blushing.

"Now what?" he inquired.

She smiled, a lovely, radiant smile. "Now we dance."

Eight

_____

From the basket of necessities Holly had brought to the circle, she withdrew an unlikely object—a small, battery-operated tape recorder. She switched it on to a recording of what sounded like Native American music. There was a flute, low and sensuous, and drums. Slowly, eyes closed, Holly began to move to the music, her motions subtle at first, delicate.

Skye watched her, feeling like a voyeur. Holly seemed totally absorbed. As far as he could tell, she wasn't peeking to see whether he was dancing, too.

He didn't intend to. But the music was irresistible and his feet began to move, of their own volition, in tempo with hers. As the drumbeats became more rapid, Skye circled the fire toward her, only to find her circling away. She's peeking, he thought, amused. And almost as soon as he thought it, her eyes came open, she looked directly into his and smiled once again.

"Come on," she said, "you're too stiff. Loosen up. Feel the music. Move your whole body."

"I can't. I feel silly."

"Nonsense."

She threw him another grin, a challenge this time. A dare. She beckoned with her fingers, but danced backward as he attempted to approach. She tossed her head and whirled away from him, turning her back. Then she faced him again and her hips were swaying rhythmically to the music, making his belly clench and his throat go dry.

Swallowing hard, Skye raised his arms over his head. He gave a jerk of his hips, more a bump and grind than anything resembling the subtle and sinuous motion she was making. But to his delight, she laughed and imitated him, bumping and grinding herself, the earth goddess transformed into the wanton.

Skye forgot how silly he felt to be dancing around a campfire in the middle of the night. Pulse racing, the turmoil in the pit of his stomach growing crazier every second, he swayed, inching closer to her, using his body as an instrument to signal his desire. To the insistent rhythms of the Indian drums, he made the same type of movements he yearned to be making in a dark place with her, naked, in her arms.

Her answering movements were everything that he could have wished—sexy, seductive, promising. If only

there were no distance between them ... if only she
didn't scoot away every time he came near enough to
touch her.

Once his fingers brushed the many-colored sash that
she had twirled around her waist, but the next sway of
her hips jerked it out of his hand. Another time,
whirling around in a tiny circle, her hair arced back
and touched his face, wafting a light, erotic fragrance. She was nimble on her feet and oh so quick at
escaping him. But there was more to it than that. She
was a goddess and he a mere mortal. He wasn't certain he *could* catch her.

The courtship dance had taken them a few yards
away from the fire, to the place where the clearing
ended and the forest reclaimed its own. Smiling,
swaying, flirting with him brazenly now, Holly didn't
seem aware that she was inches from backing into the
trunk of an enormous oak. But Skye saw it. He made
a sudden lunge and as she ducked away, her shoulders came up against the obstruction and she was
trapped.

The thrill of conquest flooded him as he took the
last step necessary to fix her there, between his body
and the ancient tree. He stilled her twitching hips with
his own. When her hands came up, he seized them at
the wrists and pinned them together over her head,
leaving one of his own hands free to touch her flushed
cheeks, her parted lips, her throat, her collarbone, her
sweet, sweet breasts.

The goddess was cornered, but she didn't protest.
When he kissed her, she moaned deep in her throat.

The kiss she gave him in return was desperate, hungry. It told him, to his delight, that desire was mutual. The combined magic of the night, the woods, the ceremonial fire and the dancing had swept away her fears.

Carefully, he drew her away from the tree, kissing her passionately as he moved. Sliding one arm down to the back of her thighs, he swung her off her feet, then bent, kneeling on one knee, and laid her on the ground just a few feet from the fire. He watched her eyes for a distress signal, but saw only welcome there.

Her lips were slightly parted, her breathing was quick and shallow, and her long, dark hair was spread out in a mantle around her slender body, sweeping the ground on one side, falling down across her breasts in the front. He yearned to brush it aside so he could touch her. He yearned to lie naked in her arms, with only her hair cloaking them both.

He eased down beside her. She shifted her hips to the side to make room for him. Her eyes were dreamy. Maybe she was still a little drunk from the ceremony, the dancing. Maybe she didn't know what was happening.

"Holly? You okay?"

"Yes, yes," she whispered.

He leaned over and kissed her mouth. When it opened sweetly under his, he accepted the silent invitation. He explored her gently with the tip of his tongue, feeling little shocks of arousal in his groin as her tongue daintily jabbed at his. He trailed his fingers from her throat to her collarbone, sliding them into the open vee of her blouse until he encountered the first button. Leaving it fastened, he pressed his palm lightly on her breast, sighing in wonder at her softness. She made a faint sound in the back of her throat, which he interpreted as encouragement.

"I'm going to make love to you," he told her.

She didn't answer, but her spine arched yearningly as he found her nipple with his fingertips. He pinched lightly, rubbed, rolled. She made another, more frantic sound, and Skye ached with the pressure that was building inside him. His skin felt hot, and he could hear his own breathing growing harsher, more impatient.

Shifting quickly, he stretched out beside her—on her, really, while simultaneously deepening the kiss. She moved beneath him, but he sensed it was more an attempt to get comfortable than a protest. Hell, it was too late for protests.

"Hol, are you sure?" His voice sounded hoarse and strange, not like him at all.

"Yes." Am I? she wondered. How had this escalated out of control? Skye's big body was covering hers, and even now he was moving to adjust the fit, tighten the mold. It was happening so fast, and it felt so good. Oh, yes, lovely, wonderful.

He kissed her hard, his tongue probing deeply and rhythmically, imitating the act of love. She responded with more joy and passion than she would have thought possible. This was right, she sensed. Here in the forest, by the light of the fire, in the lap of the goddess, Skye Rawlins was the perfect mate for her.

And then his weight was no longer upon her as he rose to remove his clothes. Her eyes focused on the bare flesh of his chest shining in the light from the moon that was illuminating the forest. Such a nice body, she thought as she watched his hands rip at the fastening of his jeans. She could see that his hands were restless and his skin alive with sweat.

I'm not afraid, she thought, in wonder. There is no darkness here.

He looked down, smiling. "Now you, my lovely goddess. I want you—what do you witch women call it—skyclad?"

"Nude in the forest? Skyclad, yes." Sitting up, she slipped her shoulders out of her blouse, and as she raised her arms, Skye knelt down beside her to help her, lifting the fabric over and off her head.

Again, he caressed her breasts, his thumbs rubbing lightly over her nipples, which were poking as hard as pebbles and supersensitive against the confines of her bra. Involuntarily, she released a moan. "D'you often go skyclad, woodland lady?" he asked.

"No, I never—"

"Never?" His hands were at her waist now, impatient, sliding her long peasant skirt down over her hips and thighs. She kicked it away, as impatient now as he. She was left wearing only the bra and a matching pair of bikini panties. "God, you're beautiful," he said.

Still feeling wild and wanton, infused with the full generative ecstasy of the goddess, Holly rocked to the music that was still beating through the forest, the sound of Native American flutes drumming, seeming to rise up out of the earth itself. Shaking her long, thick hair back over her shoulders, she reached behind her and unclipped the bra, freed herself and tossed it away.

Skye's low whistle as her breasts came into view added to her excitement. She rose up on her knees, her body still gracefully swaying, and looked directly into his rapt face as she grasped the waistband of her panties and slid them down her legs.

He was on her before she could get them entirely off, his movements quick and jerky, his breathing hard. She heard the tear of fragile cloth as he disposed of her panties and flung them after her bra; then she was flat on the ground, her heart thumping against her spine, sending its energy deep into Mother Earth, and he was with her, above her, between her thighs.

As their loins melded, she could feel how aroused he was, and the knowledge of this penetrated right through to her bones. He was kissing her—Oh, his kisses—and stroking her breasts, murmuring something low and sexy in her ear, and now he was touching her with his fingers, slowly, sensuously, making her ready. His body moved with hers, creating a jungle rhythm, a timeless beat of chest against chest, belly against belly, thigh against thigh. Then he was inside her, loving her, round and round, over and over, until the whole of her awareness was concentrated in her root chakra where the crimson light glows.

"Skye?" she whispered, fighting it for a second, reaching for control. She was both dismayed and excited to find it beyond her.

"Come with me," he murmured. "Yes, darlin'. That's it. Come with me. Come."

His voice was sexy with command, irresistible. Caught up in the tender violence of desire, she obeyed, opening to him, trusting him, accepting him. She echoed his thrusts with her own, rolling with him, pinned on a languorous wheel of sensuality, spinning up and up, higher and higher until, with a stab of wonder and delight, she shattered, keening out her pleasure in a series of breathless cries.

"Yes," she heard him whisper. "Oh, yes, my woodland goddess, yes." Then he stiffened and shuddered, and his whisper turned to a loud and timeless moan.

Afterward they lay in silence clinging to each other, while their heartbeats slowed and their breathing eased back into a normal rhythm. The tape must have come to an end, for the drumming had stopped and all was still, except for the gentle murmur of dry autumn leaves and the other less audible, more mysterious rustlings of night.

At length, Skye shifted, saying, "Holly, are you all right?"

"Oh, yes." I'm free, she added in her mind. Through the miracle of heartfelt passion, Willy Hess was gone.

"I must be heavy. You must have pebbles and twigs and heaven-knows-what poking at your lovely skin."

"No, I'm okay," she answered, smiling. "I'm wonderful."

He pushed up and dropped a kiss on the end of her upturned nose. "I was just thinking the same thing."

"It's a blessing to the earth, you know," she said dreamily. "What we just did."

"Yeah?"

"In ancient times the traditional night for this was Beltane—May Day eve. Men and women would gather in the woods and the fields to celebrate the first sproutings of green as the earth renewed itself and came awake after the long winter. They would dig holes deep into the earth, the feminine, receptive partner, into which they would drive the maypole, symbol of the acting, penetrating power of the male."

"Right," Skye said, laughing.

"After which they would attach colored ribbons to the maypole and, holding them, dance around it, creating a braid down the maypole that symbolized the miraculous web of life that springs from the union of male and female. And then, of course, after dancing themselves into a state of high passion and ecstasy, they would choose a partner and fling themselves to the earth to make love."

"Sounds good to me. Those early pagans sure knew how to have a good time. All I hope is," he added, casting a suspicious look at the ground that was now supporting his naked backside, "that those poison ivy plants did indeed comply with your request to move to another site. Otherwise, you and I may be regretting this a couple of days from now."

"If we regret it, I imagine it'll be for other reasons than poison ivy," she said solemnly.

He pulled her into his lap and hugged her. The fragrance of her hair made him dizzy with delight. "I won't regret it. You're my wife, Holly. Really and truly now. And I'll be damned if that doesn't make me—the old marriage dodger—feel terrific."

"Me, too," she admitted, her face pressed against his throat. "Skye?" she said a few moments later.

"Um?"

With a hint of laughter in her tone, she said, "What are you going to tell your suspicious townsfolk about my strange, nocturnal activities in the forest?"

"Well, I guess I'll just have to assure Roy Galleger and any other killjoys, that their sheriff has checked out the matter, done some thorough research and all, and discovered that nothing goes on at these midnight meetings except a little, uh, good, clean fun. You know—gather around a bonfire, sing a couple songs. I'll convince 'em that you and your friends are just a bunch of grown-up Girl Scouts."

"Think they'll believe you?"

"If they don't, it's into the slammer for them. Anyway, I exaggerated the complaints a bit," he admitted. "There's not that much gossip. Fact is, I wanted an excuse to come out here myself and watch."

Holly nodded as if she'd suspected it. "You're a sly devil, Sheriff Rawlins."

"Ah-hah! You are a witch. Consorting with the devil around a blazing fire."

She laughed and caressed his dark hair. "And you. That night when you rode out of the forest on your coal-black stallion, you certainly looked the part."

"I'll play it, too," he said with an exaggerated leer, "soon as I get you home. Come on." He reached out to gather up their clothes. "Let's go. Now that we've blessed the earth, I'd like to transfer my diabolical power to a nice, comfortable bed, thank you very much."

Holly dressed, then used rocks and dirt to extinguish the sacred fire. But before doing so, Skye saw her blow another prayer into her hands and into the low-burning coals. He wondered what she was wishing for, whether it concerned him, and if it would be granted.

As the last red spark went out and darkness gathered around them, he felt an atavistic chill. He and Holly had crossed a border tonight. There could be no going back, but as for what lay ahead, that he couldn't guess.

Nine

"**I**'m going hunting today," Skye said early one morning a couple of weeks later. Holly was still in bed, not fully awake, her mind, as always during those moments between sleep and wakefulness, hazy with fantasy. She was reliving the previous night's love-making with Skye...their naked limbs entwined, flesh hot, eager and tireless. His husky voice whispering sensual commands; her laughter as she complied.

"Want to come?" he asked.

"Mmm, yes, I want to come," she replied, half asleep still.

He was standing there beside the bed, grinning down at her. There was a familiar glint in his blue eyes that spoke of pleasure and promises.... "Hunting," he said again, more loudly. "Don't try to tempt me into anything else, you witch woman, you. I'm taking Barny and going pheasant hunting. Jake was going to come along with us but something came up. I can hunt alone, but I'd prefer a partner. I know how much you hate and despise hunters, but I thought I'd ask."

"Throwing down the gauntlet, huh? What if I surprise you and pick it up?"

"I'd be delighted. It's high time you learned to put aside some of your idiotic knee-jerk liberalism."

Her eyes came fully open. "Ah! Your political views aren't much different from mine, as far as I can tell, except for this one issue."

"All animals are hunters. Even you. Each time you dig up a dandelion for its roots, you're taking a life."

"As you never tire of pointing out," she said good-naturedly. She pushed the hair—and the sleep—from her eyes. "You're such a nitpicker."

Grinning, he pulled the curtains away from the windows, making her groan because the sky was still dark, with only the faintest glimmering of dawn showing. "Come on, gorgeous. Rise and shine."

"Surely even the pheasants aren't awake yet," she complained, reaching for the warm flannel robe that was hanging from the bedpost.

"You're coming, then?" he sounded surprised.

"Only because there are a few last plants I need to gather before the winter settles in. Before," she added acidly, "they die a natural death."

"I'll get breakfast ready while you dress. Wear plenty of layers. It's a cold sport."

"Coldhearted," she muttered as she stumbled toward the bathroom.

Standing in front of the mirror a few minutes later, brushing out her hair, Holly tried to figure out why she'd accepted his invitation. The hunting season was in full swing now in the area; everyday she could hear shotguns booming in the distance. Her natural, self-protective instinct was to avoid the woods and the open fields during what she considered to be this most dangerous time of the year for anything that lived and breathed. Skye had already hunted several times with his friends, coming home with game that he had cleaned and cooked, which she had refused to eat. So far, though, she refrained from quarreling with him about it. She was too much in love.

She couldn't remember a time in her adult life when she had been more happy or fulfilled. The marriage, entered into with such reluctance and trepidation, was working better than either of them could have dreamed. Their ease and compatibility had been apparent even before that passionate night in the forest, and with the collapse of the physical barriers between them, their emotional bonding had been all the more dramatic and secure.

What had seemed at the start an attraction of opposites had proved to be the sympathetic vibrations of two souls who were far more akin to one another than either of them had supposed. Holly felt certain now that they had known each other before, in former lives. Their ability to communicate without words, sensing each other's moods, reading each other's minds, proved, to her way of thinking, the strong affinity between their inner selves.

Best of all, her anxieties about sex had turned out to be groundless. Their lovemaking was joyous, passionate, playful, fun. Skye was an ardent, yet considerate lover, who took great care to do everything possible to heighten her pleasure . . . and his own.

If there was any shadow on her contentment, it lay in her dreams, which, at times, were twisted and frightening. Skye had held her and comforted her on several occasions when she'd awakened, sobbing and trembling, her heart a-thunder, her skin slick with sweat. She could never remember more than a few jagged images from the dreams, but she knew where they came from and what they were inspired by. She knew, but had chosen to forget.

"Someday, you're going to have to deal with it," her therapist in Sedona had told her. "You may be right that now isn't the time, but sooner or later the moment will come. Denial can be an excellent coping mechanism, but it almost always gives way to fear and anger and, eventually, acceptance."

Denial. Well, as Skye would probably say, "Hell, whatever works."

It wasn't until Holly had showered and nearly finished dressing that she began to regret her decision to accompany her husband hunting. Could she cope with it, she wondered, if his hunt was, by his standards, successful? How would it feel to watch him bring down his prey?

So far, by concentrating on Skye the lover, Skye the warm, charming and affectionate husband, she had managed to ward off any images of Skye the hunter. Skye the killer of small, innocent animals. Skye who pursued and cornered his prey. Skye with blood on his hands.

She shivered, as deep inside her, something stirred. Don't go. Tell him you're ill, you've changed your mind, anything. But don't be at his side when he kills.

"Oh, for goodness sake, get a grip," she said out loud.

She had to do this. Skye had come into the woods with her on the night of the last full moon in an attempt to understand her love of plants and of nature. He had joined her celebration. He had not mocked. Together, they had danced. Their lovemaking had been a sacred thing, blessed by the earth, the moon, the stars. He had accepted her, all that she was. Now it was up to her to try to understand and accept him. Skye Rawlins. Husband. Hunter.

"We're not hunting in the forest?" she asked when Skye parked his Jeep on the shoulder of a dirt road that led toward a large, open meadow.

"Not for pheasants," he reminded her as they clambered out and went around to unload the truck. Barny leaped about inside, eager and excited, whining to get out. "If I were hunting ruffed grouse, which I love to do, I'd seek them in a hardwood forest with hilly terrain. I'd take my 20-gauge Parker for that. But for pheasant hunting I've brought this 12-gauge,

double-barreled Winchester." He removed his shotgun from its case as he spoke, handling it gently, with
reverence.

Holly made a face. Men and their guns.

Skye let Barny loose. He bounded joyously out of
the Jeep and erupted into the field. Skye whistled for
him and the dog stopped short, looked back, looked
out into the tempting meadow and, with obvious reluctance, came when Skye called him again.

The purpose of the dog, Holly knew, was not only
to sniff out the birds, but to corner them and, at the
right moment, make them fly. Because Barny was a
young animal in his first season of hunting, Skye explained that things weren't going to go as smoothly as
they would with a more experienced dog.

"He's eager to please, and he knows, instinctively,
what he's supposed to do, but he doesn't entirely understand how to work as a team. He's liable to make
some mistakes."

"What sort of mistakes?"

"This gun has a range of about forty yards. If Barny
flushes a pheasant at a distance beyond that, I won't
be able to hit him."

"Too bad."

Skye hefted the shotgun, then stuffed the pockets of
his hunting jacket with more shells. "Put that orange
vest on, Holly, and we'll begin."

"I can't wait," she said, the sarcasm a little heavier
this time. But when Skye gave her a sour look, she felt
ashamed of herself. She was supposed to be going
about this with an open mind.

"Look. If you'd rather stay in the Jeep—"

"No. I'm sorry, Skye. I promised myself I wouldn't be this way. It's just that—well, this is difficult for me."

"I know. And I appreciate the fact that you're even trying to understand. Look, will you be sure to keep in mind everything I told you about gun safety?"

She nodded. He'd given her a thorough lecture on the subject during the drive.

"Make sure to stay behind me. And if you hear the sound of a bird being flushed, stand still, don't move. Don't, whatever happens, run toward it or do anything that might put you into my line of fire."

"Not likely," she said with a grimace. "Last thing I want is for you to shoot me by mistake." She nodded to his shotgun. "Aren't you going to load it?"

"I was just about to. Watch. And stop glaring at it as if it were a snake."

"I'm not. I *like* snakes."

"It's a double-barrel so it can take two shells at a time. These are the shells." He took two from his pocket and held them for her to see in the palm of his hand. "Number Four shot—that refers to the size of the pellets inside."

"The smaller the prey, the higher the number code of the shot, but the smaller the individual pellets."

He gave her a quick, reassessing glance. "I wouldn't have expected you to know that."

"Yeah, well, you'd be surprised what I know." She took the shotgun from him, broke it open, took one of the shells from his hand, loaded it in the right bar-

rel, took the second, loaded it in the left barrel, closed
the gun, then checked to be certain the safety was en-
gaged. She handed it back to him, smiling at the expression on his face.

"Well," he said after a moment. "Obviously you've
handled firearms before."

"What d'you expect? I grew up in Montana. And
I'm Tom MacLeish's granddaughter, remember?"

"Did he take you hunting?"

"If he did, it was so long ago, I've forgotten." But
as she spoke the words, something stirred inside her
again, nudging sharply, alarming her. Don't do this.
Wait in the Jeep. She closed her eyes for a moment.
No more denial, she told herself firmly. If something
was about to come back, let it come. She was tired of
all the shadows cloaking her past.

"Holly? Are you okay?"

"I'm fine. Come on, let's go."

It was a quiet morning, cool and misty with a stiff
breeze. In the east, the sun was rising with the promise of lovely weather to come. As they moved slowly
through the tall, dry grasses of the autumn meadow,
Skye turned and whispered, "This is one of the things
I love about hunting." He stopped, causing Holly
nearly to walk right into him. "Look at the sky. D'you
see the way the mist is shimmering as the sun climbs
higher? And listen to the birdsong."

"It does seem louder than usual."

"Exactly. Everything seems louder, clearer, sharper,
more distinct. That's because we're more alert. More
tuned in to our surroundings. This morning we're part

of nature. Usually we try to transcend it. But to find pheasants, you have to think like a pheasant, become a pheasant."

"Birdbrained?" she teased him.

"Seriously. Would I feel safer feeding in that clump of tall grass over there on the edge of the field, or would I rather eat down there in that hollow? If I hear the dog, which way will I run? Where can I hide? At what moment will I panic and fly? The hunter, you see, must become one with the game."

"And you laughed at me for talking to poison ivy."

"You're right," he admitted. "Maybe what you and I do is not all that different."

Maybe not, she thought. When there was a particular plant she was looking for, she tried to feel it out, sense where it would dwell, what sort of earth it would require, how much water, how much sun. She would imagine herself as a sister plant and try to communicate with the object of her seeking on some sort of psychic or cellular level. "Lead me to thee," she would chant silently, moving through forest or field almost in a trance. More often than not, she would sense nature responding, and she would find the herb she sought.

And then, with its permission, she would take it from the ground. Harvest it. Kill it. Never would she take all the plants from a given area, and never the young ones. Never, of course, would she touch a rare or endangered species, no matter how efficacious its medicinal properties might be.

Skye, she now understood, followed similar rules, as did all responsible hunters. He hunted only species whose numbers were plentiful, and exclusively during the season when hunting was allowed. Today he was seeking cock pheasants, he'd told her—the males. Most states didn't allow the hunting of hen pheasants.

"How do you know the difference?" she'd asked on the way.

"By the color of their feathers. The male has crimson markings on its cheeks."

"How can you see that if the bird suddenly flies off overhead?"

"If you can't, if there's any doubt whatsoever, you hold your fire."

So it was with plants. You took it if you needed it, but too many you did not take. You loved and respected the natural world, and you tried not to interfere too much with the natural rhythms of its cycles of life, reproduction and death.

"There," said Skye, pointing, his voice low and excited. "Barny's picked up the scent."

Sure enough, the retriever was running around, back and forth in front of a long, narrow patch of briars, wagging his tail and whining. "He's making game," said Skye, beckoning to Holly as he moved through the tall grass, his shotgun at the port arms position. "Hurry. We're almost out of range."

Holly followed, startled to find that her own adrenaline was pumping. As much as Skye or Barny, she wanted to find that bird. There was something deeply primitive, instinctive almost, about being hot on its trail.

"The birds have been feeding in the grass, but now they're retreating into the thicker stuff," Skye whispered. He had slowed to a quiet, careful walk now that they had come up a few yards behind the excited dog, who was looking for a way through the briars to get at the birds. "They'd rather run than fly, but they'll fly if they think there's no alternative."

"Where is it?' she mouthed as he stopped and remained motionless, watching Barny.

"There. Wait. Any second now."

Barny looked back, wagged his tail harder, then turned and plunged into the briars. Skye raised the shotgun to his shoulder even before the clap of wings. Three things happened simultaneously: he identified the bird as male and fair game, he took aim, and his finger froze on the trigger as he envisioned the expression that would cloud Holly's face when the bird tumbled from the sky.

The pheasant flew on, and Skye's gun barrel followed, but in a split second the shot changed from easy to difficult. A moment later and the damn thing was out of range.

He lowered the shotgun. Barny, clearly confused, looked back toward his master, as if to say, "Hey, what happened? There was supposed to be a boom and that bird was supposed to fall down and I was supposed to run and fetch it. I did my job. Why didn't you do yours?"

But Holly threw back her head and laughed. She whirled and enveloped him in a hug. "Thank you, Skye. You could have killed him, I know. But he was beautiful. Thank you for letting him live."

He felt suddenly, unaccountably angry. What the hell had happened to him? He should have taken the shot. Why hadn't he pulled the trigger?

"It was the wrong thing to do. Damn! I confused the dog. It was unfair to him." And to me, he was thinking. And even to you, Holly MacLeish.

He'd invited her along because, well, things had gotten to a certain point with them—the point where, to his mind, you either moved closer or you moved apart. He'd wanted her to see this primitive, elemental side of his nature. He wanted her to understand it. More importantly, he wanted her to accept him for the man that he was.

There was no chance of that now. Look at her, still smiling, still happy. She thinks she knows me, but she's wrong.

If he had been alone, that bird would have been supper.

He stalked off to find Barny, to praise and reassure him. Never should have brought her, he was thinking. Never will again.

Fifteen minutes later, Barny was into another bird, and this time Skye didn't hesitate. He moved quickly in the wake of the dog, leaving Holly behind, making no attempt to wait or explain or palliate the experience for her. This is me, he felt like shouting at her. I love hunting. Dammit, this is who I am.

More intelligently than he'd expected, Barny cast a glance back to make sure his master was following before forging ahead into the newest path of briars. "Good boy," Skye muttered. "You got potential."

When the cock pheasant flew this time, Skye already had the shotgun to his shoulder. It was smooth and sure, like a thousand times before, perfect. The arc of the creature's flight, the swing of the gun, the gentle squeezing of the trigger and the sudden cartwheeling plunge of the bird from the sky, carefully observed by both the dog and his master.

Even before the body hit the ground, Barny was after it, and for several moments both bird and dog disappeared in the thigh-high meadow grasses. Then Barny came bounding back, the bird held gently between his widely spread jaws, his retriever instincts arrowing him to Skye, to whom, with great solemnity and pride, he presented his trophy.

"Good dog," Skye praised him, patting him and taking the bird, which was cleanly dead, thank goodness. Even seasoned hunters tended to feel a twinge of guilt over the game they did not instantly kill. "You did everything right that time, Barny boy. Last time, too, for that matter. You're a good boy."

Only then, after making an appropriate fuss over the dog, did Skye turn to Holly, who lingered several yards behind. Walking toward her, Skye could see that she was pale and stiff-limbed, and there was an unnatural shimmer in her eyes.

Staring at the dead pheasant, she slowly shook her head. "I'd like to go home now, if you don't mind."

"Fine. We've got supper. We'll go home."

"If you think I'm *eating* that—"

"You don't kill what you aren't going to eat."

"The hunter's ethic, huh?" She squared her shoulders, as if trying to control herself. "Look, I'm sorry. It's just that—when you didn't shoot the other one, I thought..." Her voice trailed off. "I don't understand you," she finally said.

He stared at her in silence. No, he thought sadly. And she probably never would.

Holly's gaze dropped again to the bird. And suddenly one hand went to her throat. She began to gasp, to choke, to point shakily at the bird, whose feathers were ruffling lightly in the stiff wind. "It's not dead," she said. "You haven't killed it, you monster, you're torturing it... it's not dead."

"Of course it's dead," said Skye, certain of that.

She was swaying. "Oh, God. Oh, God." She put her hands up to her face, covering her eyes, tearing at her hair; then she bent over, as if she were about to be sick. "They died so slowly," she whispered. "Oh, God, they took so long to die."

"Jesus." Skye dropped both the shotgun and the bird and rushed to her side just in time to support her as her legs collapsed beneath her. Clinging to him, she sank to her knees in the tall grass, moaning.

"Holly?" He knelt beside her and put his arms around her. Her skin was like ice and she was trembling all over. "Holly what's the matter? It's okay, darlin'." He was stroking her shoulders, her hair. "I've got you. I'm here, Holly, it's okay."

"Oh, Skye," she said, transforming his name into a cry of anguish. She turned her face against the zipper of his jacket and started to sob.

Ten

Holly couldn't stop crying. The tears that had begun to flow in the misty meadow had not let up all afternoon or evening. At times she sobbed, but mostly she sat still, in silence, allowing the moisture to trickle down her cheeks.

The loss of control was almost as terrifying as the shocking surge of memory that had caused it. Holly had always prided herself on her emotional strength and fortitude.

All day long Skye had tried to get her to talk about it, share what she was feeling. Give him an explanation. Free him from what she could see in his ravaged countenance was a heavy burden of guilt and responsibility.

But every time she tried, she could not choke out the words. What words were there to speak the unspeakable?

It wasn't until nine o'clock that evening, when he picked up the phone and tried to call Jake, the physician, for help, that Holly found the words to stop him.

"No, Skye, please. I don't need a doctor. I'll be all right."

"Honey, you've been crying all day. You're frightening me."

"I need to cry. Don't try to stop me. There are millions of tears to be shed."

"But what are you crying for?"

"For all the little birds and animals," she whispered, and lost it again.

"I haven't killed that many," she heard him say, sounding both concerned and exasperated.

"Not you," she managed. "Not you, Skye."

"Who, then, for God's sake?"

The words emerged in a sibilant whisper. "Willy Hess."

"I figured as much," he told her with a sigh. "You want to tell me about it?"

She shook her head. "I can't. I can't."

"You remembered something?"

"Yes. Oh, God, yes."

"Something else that happened, something you repressed?"

"I can't talk about it. I just can't."

He was sitting beside her on the bed. He slid one arm around her shoulders, drew her close. She huddled stiffly, not able to relax, even in his arms. "Listen, sweetheart. There's nothing you can't tell me. Whatever it is, you'll feel better, getting it out."

"Someday. Tomorrow maybe. Not tonight."

"Tomorrow, then. I'm not going to hassle you, hon. Are you hungry? Tired? You want to sleep?"

"Yes," she whispered. "Please. Hold me. Help me sleep."

He stripped and got in bed beside her, held her, put out the light. "It's okay, babe," he whispered. "I'm here beside you. You're safe now. Go to sleep."

She woke screaming. She was tied down, helpless, she couldn't move. There was a man's body, strong, merciless, holding her down. He was going to hurt her. He had a knife....

She fought to get free, thrashing, trying to throw him off her, feeling him restrain her, screaming, screaming until a hand covered her mouth and smothered her cries....

"Shh, Holly, it's okay. It's me, hon, it's Skye. Take it easy, it's me."

The hand moved away from her mouth and she managed to cut off the next scream as full consciousness returned. He wasn't restraining her, he was holding her. In sleep, their limbs had become entangled. He wasn't trying to hurt her. He was her lover, her husband. He was Skye.

Her coiled muscles loosened and, once again, reflexive tears welled up in her eyes. "I'm sorry. I thought—I don't know—you were hurting me. I must have been dreaming.''

"I'd never hurt you, Holly. I love you."

It was the first time he'd ever said it, she realized. She'd longed to hear him say it, but until now he never had. And the words left a feeling of expectancy between them—they called for an answer, a reciprocation. "I love you, too," she was supposed to say.

Why'd he have to wait till now? she thought miserably. She wanted to say it back, but for some reason, tonight, still shaking from her nightmare, the words just stuck in her throat.

She answered him with silence.

"It's a good thing that Hess creep is already dead, or I'd be tempted to kill him myself," Skye finally said in a hollow, ravaged voice.

Holly knew then that she was going to have to tell him. She owed him the truth. If he couldn't live with it, that was something they both needed to know.

She wiped her eyes on a corner of the sheet. Then she reached over and switched on the light on the bedside table. It was not a harsh or a bright light, and for that she was grateful. She felt dirty, guilty, as if she needed to hide her face.

"What are you—"

"Skye, listen. We need to talk."

"Okay, hon. I'm listening."

"Something happened to me. Well, a lot of things happened to me, actually, some of which I'd forgotten about—repressed—until today. But some of it I hadn't forgotten. Some of it I ought to have told you about before this. But I didn't want to think about it. And telling it brings it all back.''

"Hess raped you, didn't he?" His voice was heavy.

She shook her head. "Not exactly. It's not that simple.''

Skye was wondering what the hell that meant as she sat up in bed, pushing the pillows into a bunch behind her to support her back. "There was abuse, yes, some of it sexual. It went on for a long time. Far longer than anybody realized." She stopped and was silent, almost too long for him to bear. "You see, Willy Hess was my brother."

Skye blinked. For the first time since he could remember, he was utterly shocked. "Your *brother?* What do you... I thought he was an ex-con who kidnapped you?"

"He was that, too. Of course. But he was also my brother. Well, stepbrother, really. He was my mother's second husband's son, by a former marriage. After my father died and she remarried, we went to live with them in Portland, Washington. I was nine. He was ten. We weren't blood relatives, but we were raised together for the next few years."

"My God, Holly. I had no idea."

She was hugging herself. "It was bad from the beginning. He was a strange boy and he used to frighten me." She laughed a little. "You may not believe this, but I wasn't easily frightened in those days, either. I was a tomboy, tough and scrappy and pretty fearless. Annie Oakley from *Annie Get Your Gun* was my heroine. I'd seen the musical one winter in New York when we'd gone there for a special trip before my father died. I knew every lyric to every song and I could recite the book by heart.

"Like my grandfather, my stepfather was a hunter. He taught us both to shoot—Willy and me. But I liked skeet shooting, just like Annie. I was a runner-up for junior state champion at the age of thirteen."

Skye opened his mouth, but no words came out. He felt like a fool, in more ways than one. No wonder she'd known how to load his shotgun.

"Willy was what is now generally recognized as a sociopath," she went on, keeping her voice deliberate and steady. "As I understand it, there's no real explanation for people like him. They haven't necessarily had rotten parents, been brutally treated, or been exposed to great loss or trauma at an early age. They seem normal on the surface, but are twisted inside."

"Like Ted Bundy."

"Exactly. Willy couldn't relate to other people's feelings. He was either unwilling or unable to empathize with anyone else's fear or pain. He was entirely wrapped up in his own gratification. This made him, well, *evil* may be the only word for it. As a human being, he lacked a vital piece."

"Surely your parents must have known," Skye said. "Couldn't they keep him away from you?"

She gave a bitter little smile. "Sociopaths can also be extremely clever. Willy's father indulged him because his mother, like my father, had been killed in a tragic accident. Divorce is common, but it's relatively unusual to be the child of a widowed parent nowadays, and the shrinks and the social workers don't always know what to expect. Both Willy and I were thought to be acting out our grief.

"What would typically happen was, he would do something horrid to me, like putting fire ants down the back of my jeans or snakes in my bed and, at first, I would fight back, scream, throw a tantrum, tell the entire story, indignantly, to my mother and stepfather. Willy would call me a liar and invent plausible stories to prove that he couldn't possibly have done the things I'd accused him of... that I was exaggerating, or even deluding myself. Our parents must have figured we were both lying. What I learned as a result was that the world was dangerous and unjust and that people wouldn't believe me. What Willy learned was that with a good story to back him up, he could get away with anything."

Skye muttered an imprecation.

"As we grew older, whatever was skewed inside him took an even nastier turn." She cleared her throat nervously. "He liked to trap small animals—mice, baby rabbits, birds, chipmunks—and torture them. And when he went hunting, he would deliberately try to injure, not kill, the bird in the air. He was an excellent shot, and he knew how to hit areas that weren't vital—he practiced it. The poor thing would fall and the dog would retrieve it, and it would still be alive and looking around. He wouldn't kill it quickly the way you're supposed to when that happens by accident. He would stand there, smiling, and watch it exhaust itself trying to escape and, very slowly, die."

Skye groaned. Her reaction this morning when she'd thought the bird he'd shot had still been alive suddenly made sense. *They died so slowly. Oh, God, they took so long to die.*

"Jesus, Holly, no wonder you feel the way you do about hunting."

"It gets worse, I'm afraid."

"Tell me."

She closed her eyes, hugging herself even harder. "This is the part I'd repressed. The stuff about torturing animals—that was pretty vague to me, as well. But most of this—the details—I'd forgotten, until today. Strangely enough, it came back all at once, clear, complete and coherent."

She drew a deep fortifying breath. "When I was fifteen, my mother died of cancer. My stepfather, a decent man who simply couldn't face up to the fact that there was something wrong with his son, was a successful businessman in Portland. Unfortunately, he traveled a lot, leaving me alone with Willy. My stepbrother was a year older at the time and, physically, coming into his manhood.

"He told me outright that he wanted to have sex, to see what it felt like. Trouble was, he was such a strange and hostile kid that no girls would go out with him. I was the only girl he knew. We weren't related, he pointed out to me, so why not?"

"Son of a—"

"Shh. Let me tell it without interruption. This is hard for me." She paused for a moment. "I wasn't a sophisticated teenager. I didn't know as much as kids seem to know nowadays. I'd had no serious boy-friends . . . I was basically an innocent. And blood re-lationship or no, I considered Willy my brother. In short, I was shocked and terrified by his proposal. Bursting into tears, I told him he was sick and crazy. I know in retrospect that this was exactly the reaction that pleased him most. He got off on frightening me.

"And so his campaign of terrorism began. He pur-sued me, grabbing me when I least expected it, kiss-ing me, fondling me, and so on. And every time I fought or refused or threatened to tell his father, he captured some small animal, killed it slowly, and brought me the body."

"Jesus Christ, Holly."

"I had a dog that I loved very much. A Labrador retriever named Dusty. She looked a little like Barny—shorter coat, of course. My mother had given Dusty to me shortly before her death, and she was my link with my mother, you see. Willy knew how much I loved that dog." Her fingers had tightened on the sheet, clutching it so hard, her knuckles were visible through her skin.

"If I didn't sleep with him, he informed me, he was going to torture Dusty and kill her. He described how he was going to do it, every detail. I knew he meant it. But I also knew that even if I gave in and did what he wanted, he would kill my dog sooner or later anyway, because he was crazy and getting crazier, and he ac-tually took pleasure in it. More pleasure, probably, then he would ever take in sex."

Skye reached over and took her tense hands in his. Her fingers tightened on his, the way they had on the sheet.

He wanted to say something to comfort her, but he didn't trust himself to speak. The rage inside him was monumental. It was a damn good thing Hess was already in his grave.

"On the night he had appointed for my violation, I played along with him," Holly continued. "I pretended to be eager, curious. I even cooked him a nice dinner—my stepfather was away, as usual—topped off at the end with apple pie and ice cream. He wolfed it down and swallowed a cup of strong coffee with the dessert, as I hoped he would. Into the coffee I had crushed five of the sleeping pills my mother used to take to help her get through her nights of pain when her cancer spread."

"Good for you," Skye said tightly. He wanted to hug her for her courage, but once again, his emotions were too intense. She was in a fragile state, telling this story, and he didn't want to do anything that might frighten or distract her.

"I waited, terrified that it hadn't been enough. When he finally passed out, I took Dusty and put her into my stepfather's car—which I barely knew how to drive since I didn't yet have my license—and fled. I drove all night and all the next day, not daring to stop. I drove all the way to Montana, where I sought refuge with my grandfather. I told him the whole story and, thank God, he believed me. He went to court, and after months of legal wrangling, he was able to get custody of me, partly because, in the meantime, Willy had graduated from animals to human beings and was convicted for assaulting a girl in Portland.

"He was in and out of prison for the next few years—mostly in, because his crimes were always violent and sadistic. They finally put him away for life, no chance of parole, and I tried to put it behind me, excise the whole nasty experience from my life. And I succeeded, for the most part. I moved to Sedona. I had boyfriends. I started my herb business. I was happy and secure."

"Until he broke out of prison," said Skye.

"Yes. And came after me. You know that story, or most of it, anyway. You asked me, was I raped, and I told you I wasn't. That was true, in the usual sense of the word. But he tied me down and—and terrorized me with his vivid descriptions of all the things he intended to do to me. He made it very real, you see. He was good at that. And he hurt me."

Skye cursed again.

"I was his obsession, you see. All the other women he attacked always looked like me—same build, same long, dark hair. Apparently he blamed me for all his problems, because I was the first female who'd rejected him. Now, finally, he told me he was going to get even. Now, finally, he was going to get what I'd refused to give him when we were kids." She was shivering all over. "He was just starting in on me when the police stormed the place. He knew it was all over. He turned the gun on himself. And the irony is that he was more merciful with himself than he'd been with anything else he'd ever killed. He put the gun to his temple and died instantly.'' She paused a moment, then added, "God forgive me, but I was glad.''

Skye had restrained himself as long as he could. He slid over in bed and pulled her down into his arms, stroking her hair, offering her his strength and his compassion. At first, she was stiff in his embrace. He could feel her trembling, hanging on desperately to her control. Then, with a suddenness that astonished him, she relaxed. And became the aggressor.

She rolled to her back and pulled him down upon her, cradling him between her thighs. Tilting back her head, she searched for his mouth, and found it. Her kiss was passionate, frantic. Her hands moved into his hair, clutching him so hard, it hurt. "I need you," she whispered. "Make love to me.''

Gladly, he thought, avidly returning her kisses. The way she'd distanced herself from him after the hunting had scared him. He'd been imagining that it was over, that she'd never let him touch her again.

"Make me forget,'' she whispered against his mouth.

This he wasn't so sure of. No one could make the past go away.

But her insistent passion excited him, and he was ready almost immediately to take her. The real surprise was that she seemed to be ready, too. He was always careful to move slowly, no matter how impatient for consummation he might be. Women, he knew, were different from men in this respect.

"Love me," she pleaded, twisting her hips, trying to find him. "I need you, Skye."

"Take it easy, love. There's plenty of time. Let me caress you for a while."

"No, dammit." Her hand slid down between their bodies, reaching for him far more boldly than ever before. She stroked him, her fingers warm and alive. "Please. I need you now."

With a groan he did her bidding, holding her still and joining their bodies with a powerful thrust. She cried out and he thought, I knew it, she wasn't ready. But it didn't stop her demands that he continue, nor her frantic efforts to accelerate his rhythms, to find release.

She was seeking oblivion, he realized. Using him, in a way. He felt oddly resentful. He wanted her, he loved her, and God knew her every movement was driving him closer and closer to the edge, but this was all wrong. This wasn't the way he wanted it to be.

He wanted her to say she loved him. He wanted to hear the words and know that they were spoken from her heart. Odd, he thought dazedly. He'd never wanted that before.

But he knew Holly wasn't thinking about love. She was using him, his body, his masculine power and strength, to fight back shadows, darkness, death.

Okay. Okay, if it worked.

But he knew a few moments later that it wasn't working. At least, not for her. He'd lost her. He could feel it. Her movements had slowed, her passion slackened, and she wasn't with him anymore.

He groaned again, knowing he was way ahead of her, and that at any second, she was going to freeze up on him or cry. He tried to withdraw, but her arms wrapped tight around his waist wouldn't let him. Then she caressed him, deeply, and he lost all control and climaxed, whispering her name.

"I'm sorry," he said, when he could speak. "I knew it wasn't right for you. I shouldn't—"

"Shh. It was fine."

"Holly—"

"I'm okay, Skye. Please don't worry about me."

But in her eyes he saw something that frightened him profoundly: a bleakness, a distance, a despair.

Eleven

"**I**'ve had a letter from my friend Moira," Holly announced one gray November morning at breakfast. "She's invited me to come down and spend a few weeks with her in Salt Lake City. They don't have much of a winter, of course, compared to Montana. Plants still grow. I'm thinking about calling her, accepting her invitation."

Skye looked up from his coffee cup. He'd been staring into it, contemplating the blackness inside. He heard Holly's words with shock, even though he'd been half expecting something like this. Day after day, night after night, she had slipped farther away from him.

"You can't do that. By the terms of Tom's will, we have to live together for six months. There are still three left."

"It seems to me that's a technicality now. I've married you. Everyone in Whittier knows that we have been living here together." She was nervously fingering the silverware, rubbing her thumb over the tines of a fork. "There's only so much that anybody can legislate about what goes on in a marriage. I'm entitled to take a vacation. I'll come back before the six months is officially up, to keep up appearances, and in March we'll be free to divide up the property and file for a divorce."

"Dammit, Holly. Who said anything about a divorce?"

"We did." She seemed to be making an effort to keep her voice calm and even. "If you remember. This was never meant to be a permanent arrangement. We married each other on the express condition that it wouldn't be."

"We married each other not knowing exactly what would happen. We agreed to wait and see."

"Well," she said, tugging nervously at a long lock of her black hair. "It's not working, is it?"

If it's not working, he thought wretchedly, it's because you're not letting it work.

It was as if the serpent had entered their garden. What had seemed such a glorious union during a few weeks of languorous, mindless, sweet and natural lovemaking, had somehow degenerated into a miserable estrangement. Gradually, they had retreated from each other. Instead of being two lovers with no clear sense of individual selves, they'd returned to being two separate and wary people, a man and a woman, a hunter and a plant lover, a killer and a healer.

The worst of it was, Skye didn't know exactly why.

Holly had remembered her past, explored it, talked about it. He had listened with sympathy and understanding, trying to show her that he loved her and that she was safe. He'd expected her to feel free now of her shadows, but that hadn't happened. Instead, it seemed the shadows were gathered around her, darker than ever.

If we get married, it's possible that my pain could somehow spread out and touch you. That's the last thing I want for you, Skye.

Unfortunately, that's exactly what had happened.

Even their lovemaking had been haunted by ghosts. Holly's attempts to lose herself in passion had become ever more futile, and for the past couple of nights she had been unwilling to even try. She'd been avoiding him, either by going to bed early or by sitting downstairs until she was sure he was asleep. In bed, she kept strictly to her own side, apologizing if she so much as bumped him in the night. When he tried to coax her back into his arms, she stiffened and slid away.

"I'm sorry," she told him over and over. "It's not your fault. It's me, Skye. It's me."

Unsteadily, Skye gulped what was left of his coffee. He had an image of her stretched out on her back, her hair tangled, her lovely bare skin damp with the exertions of lovemaking. What's happened to us? he wondered. Somehow he had failed her. Dammit, it *was* his fault.

When he was feeling most despairing, Skye could easily find reasons to blame himself. After all, he was the one who, in the past, had been infamous for his refusal to commit himself to a serious relationship. His methods of avoiding intimacy had been extensive and varied, some of them unrecognized by him until enough time had passed for him to gain perspective. More than one lover had accused him of distancing himself from an affair without even being aware of what he was doing.

Maybe, he thought now, I wanted it this way. Maybe, on some unconscious level, I planned it. Maybe I'll be happy when she leaves.

The truth was, until he'd taken Holly hunting and shot that pheasant, things had been going almost too well between them. Now that harmony was shattered. It was as if he could only get so close to a woman before he began to feel a perverse desire to sabotage the relationship.

He had killed, and she had turned away in disgust. He must have known in his heart that it would happen. Hell, even if there had never been a psychopathic stepbrother in her past, she'd made no secret of her dislike for hunters, and he'd insisted on throwing it in her face.

Served him right if she could no longer stomach making love.

Trouble with this scenario, he reminded himself, is that he *wasn't* going to be happy if she left.

I love her, dammit. I don't want her to go.

"Holly? Are you really giving up on us? Is that what you're telling me?"

Almost imperceptibly, she shrugged. "I need to get away," she said softly. "Maybe if I have some time alone, some time to think, some time to work things out..." Her voice trailed off.

He longed to reach out and touch her, hold her, just hold her, but things had deteriorated so far between them that it didn't seem possible anymore. If she left, at least there would be an end to this tension. Relief from the necessity of having to be restrained and polite with the person you wanted to...to sweep into your arms and carry up to bed.

"It's not just the hunting, is it? It's the lovemaking, as well."

She bit her lower lip, her face drawn, her green eyes bright.

"Don't you feel...don't you enjoy—"

"That's not it," she interrupted, shaking her head now, hard. "I keep telling you, it's not you. Making love with you has always been beautiful, magical. More than that. To me it's been a miracle, Skye."

"Until recently," he said dryly.

"Since I remembered about Willy, I feel so...I don't know—so paralyzed."

"There are people in this area you can talk to, experts who can help you work this through. Do whatever you need to do to get your head straightened out, but do it here, in Montana, with me. We don't have to sleep together if it's too difficult for you right now. I can wait. But if you leave me, if you run away to Salt Lake City, I'm afraid you'll never come back.''

"Skye, you're so good to me. You always have been. But you don't understand.'' She blinked away a tear. "It's difficult for me to be with you.''

"What do you mean? Why?''

"I never should have gone hunting with you.''

"Yeah, well, we can't change what's happened. And sooner or later you were going to have to deal with that side of my nature.''

"I wish you didn't look like him,'' she said in a barely audible voice.

"What?''

She gnawed on her bottom lip. "Nothing.''

"I look like Willy Hess?''

"A little,'' she admitted. "Tall, dark, something similar about your mouth, your jaw—''

"Dammit, Holly! I understand that you're having problems relaxing and allowing yourself to trust me—or any man. Hell, that's natural. But what I can't understand is why you almost seem to identify me with this pervert. That drives me wild.''

She made a helpless gesture with her hands. "It's not something rational. It goes very deep. You're like him physically, you represent the legal system, which was incapable of protecting me from him...'' her voice dropped very low ''...you want sex from me, as did he.''

"I'm your husband," he said tersely. "I'm not some raving maniac. I want to give you pleasure. But I would never, ever hurt you. Surely you know that."

"Of course I do. But you're a hunter. You hurt birds and animals. You kill them. Don't you see, after what he put me through, there's no way around that for me. I thought maybe there was. I thought I could cope with it, come to understand it, but now I know I can't. Forgive me, but it's impossible for me."

He rose, flinging his chair backward so hard it nearly fell over. He paced across the kitchen, once, twice. "So what do we do, Holly? Where do we go from here? Are you asking me to change? I can't give up hunting, I've done it all my life. As a law-enforcement officer, with criminals, it's part of my livelihood. Seeking, hunting, giving chase. Don't you see, it's who I am."

"Yes, I do see. Of course I don't want you to change. You're who you are, and I respect that. But I'm who I am, and maybe the two just aren't compatible."

"We are compatible, dammit! We've lived together all this time with scarcely a ripple of conflict or discontent, except for this hunting business. You're the first woman I've ever spent so much time with who hasn't driven me nuts."

He stopped pacing beside her chair, placing a hand upon her shoulder. When she would have turned her face away, he cupped her chin and forced her to look at him. "Holly, I love you. Let's try to work things out."

Her lower lip was trembling as she answered, "And I care for you, too, Skye, very much."

I care for you. Not, I love you.

"But I can't live with you. We have to accept that this isn't going to work. We have to be honest with each other. We have to end it."

"Dammit!" The flat of his hand slammed down on the top of the table, setting the dishes clattering. "I'm not willing to accept that this is the end."

Her voice flattened. "Neither was my brother Willy."

Skye could feel himself whiten. "No matter what I say, what I do, you seem to be able to see him in me. Well, that's your sickness, Holly, your poison. If you don't face up to it, the rest of your life will be truly wretched. Because you'll see him in everyone. Maybe the next guy won't be a hunter, but he'll have some other quality that reminds you of Willy, and you won't be able to love him, either, or live with him. And that's the way it'll be, again and again, forever. Every time you snatch at happiness, old Willy's ghost will be there, laughing at you. And he'll have defeated you, after all, won't he?" Moving closer, he gripped her shoulders between his palms. "Won't he, dammit?"

"Let go of me!"

"I love you, Holly. Look at me, damn you, when I say that. I love you."

She pulled away, crying. "I'm sorry" was all she could manage in response.

Skye thrust her away from him, feeling the tears well in his own eyes. Blindly, he strode into his study, jerked a shotgun from the glass case and jammed a few shells into his trousers' pocket. He grabbed his jacket and his shooting vest from the hook near the front door as he yelled for Barny.

"Skye—" Holly's voice was wavering, wretched.

"Do what you have to do," he told her. "I can't stay here and try to deal with this any longer. I'm at my limit. I can't take any more."

"Skye, you sound so despairing. You're not—you won't—"

"I'm not going to hurt myself, if that's what you're worried about," he retorted. "I'm going to murder a few birds instead."

"Skye, please don't leave me like this."

"You've got it wrong, Holly. You're the one who's leaving me. You're the one who's running away from all your problems, as if that were going to solve them."

With Barny at his heels, he went through the door. He stopped for a moment on the threshold to add, "Where's the strong and passionate earth goddess, afraid of nothing, who danced her way into my heart? Where is she, Holly? That's what I'd like to know."

Then he was gone, slamming the door behind him.

Twelve

After Skye left, Holly sat motionless at the kitchen table for what must have been close to an hour. He was right, she kept thinking. Skye was absolutely right about her, and completely justified in his anger.

Her heart clenched at the memory of his deepening expression of despair. He hadn't realized until this morning how serious the rift between them had grown. He hadn't guessed the extent of her confusion and her fear. He'd thought, the way men do, that he could conquer it. And protect her. Make the past go away, make everything all right.

Oh, God, if only he could!

But that was something only she could do. And she had to do it on her own.

Rousing herself, Holly climbed the stairs to the bedroom she had been sharing with Skye, intending to pack a few things and get out of here before he returned from hunting. She wouldn't go to Moira in Salt Lake, she decided. He was right that it would be too much like running away. She'd go to a motel instead. Someplace where she could be alone with herself and her demons. Someplace where she could go inside and meditate and find the answer to his final question, *Where's the strong and passionate earth goddess, afraid of nothing, who danced her way into my heart?*

Opening the closet, she removed a suitcase from the top shelf and took it over to the bed. But the thought of packing defeated her. Instead she pushed the suitcase aside and lay down, stretching herself out full length on the bed. It was here, she thought, that she and Skye had loved each other, whispered, laughed, urged, joined. She remembered a night when, both a little drunk with their desire for each other, they'd spontaneously played an erotic game.

It had begun downstairs, underneath the mammoth stag's head in the living room. Skye had lunged at her, and she'd slipped out of his grip and spun away. Laughing, she had put the sofa between them, then ducked behind a big chair. When he tripped over the coffee table in his attempt to catch her, she'd run out of the living room and up the stairs to the second floor.

He had come after her, of course, cursing good-naturedly. And stalked her as she'd fled from room to room. Knowing the old house much better than he did, she had finally concealed herself in an alcove in an unused bedroom, and Skye had no luck at all in finding her until he'd called Barny in to help.

"Where's Holly, boy? Find Holly," he'd ordered, and the golden retriever, nose sniffing, tail wagging, had promptly led his master to the place where she was crouching, her heart pounding, her blood rioting in her veins.

"Not fair!" she'd protested as he'd dragged her out of her lair.

"Gotcha!" he'd crowed, and clamping one wrist in a grip that felt as steely as his sheriff's department handcuffs, he'd led her in triumph to their bed, where he had made rough love to her while she, unafraid, had keened out her pleasure.

During this entire episode, she reflected now, it had never for a moment occurred to her to fear him. She hadn't confused Skye with her dead stepbrother. No dark memories had surfaced to dampen her excitement, nor her subsequent delight.

Why not? she asked herself.

The answer exploded upon her. At the deepest level of her being, she trusted Skye.

Where there was trust, there could be love.

Maybe it was not hopeless, after all.

As Holly rose from the bed, uncertain now whether to stay or go, she noticed the white flakes dancing past the window. Snow. In southern Arizona where she had lived for so long it was a rare and unusual sight. Even here—winters were brutal, yes, but did it usually snow so hard so early? It was coming down heavily. Probably just a squall. Did it mean Skye would be home soon? Could one hunt in a snowstorm?

Come home, a voice inside her whispered. Come home and stop me from leaving you. The truth is, my darling, I don't think I really want to go.

Out in the woods with Barny, his shotgun cradled across his body in the port arms position so it could readily be lifted to his shoulder and fired, Skye paid little attention to the snow. Usually, he was careful about the weather. A hunter had to be. The dangers of hypothermia were too severe, particularly in the high country of Montana where the temperature could drop dramatically in just a few minutes. But today he was heedless.

He and Barny had flushed a couple of birds in the first hour of hunting, but he'd failed to bring any down. Lately, though, they'd had no luck in finding game. After a couple more hours of tramping, feeling the temperature dive, the wind accelerate, the moisture from the precipitation soak his clothes, his shotgun get heavier and all the ruffed grouse, apparently, taken shelter from the storm, Skye's enthusiasm for hunting dwindled. The words to an ancient folk song began repeating themselves over and over in his brain.

Western wind, when wilt thou blow,
The small rain down can rain?
Christ, if my love were in my arms,
And I in my bed again!

This desire so occupied him that it wasn't until the wind had turned biting and the snow was beginning to clog his footsteps that Skye stopped and whistled for Barny, who came bounding back toward him through the thickening snow.

"Good boy," he praised him as Barny came to his side and sat. His golden coat was matted with dampness, but he was still happily wagging his tail. "Not much luck today, huh? Come on. Weather's turned nasty. We'd better head back."

As he reversed their direction, Barny looked faintly disgusted, but was soon running ahead again, avidly sniffing for any scents he might have missed. He had run ahead, around a bend, out of sight and off the path, when Skye heard an ominous metallic snap, followed by a loud whine of canine agony. Horrified, he knew what the sound must be. Barny must have stepped into a trap left carelessly and illegally in the woods by a less scrupulous hunter.

This was exactly what he found—Barny, confused and frantic, startled yelps of pain issuing from his throat as he jerked at his imprisoned leg, raw and bleeding, locked within the rusty jaws of an ugly leg-hold trap.

Skye felt a swift, ferocious anger at whoever had done this. Ranchers occasionally set traps for coyotes and other predators, and Skye had heard rumors of a wolf in the vicinity, who had been raiding farmers' livestock. But it was illegal to hunt wolves with a rifle, much less a trap.

Fighting back his fury for Barny's sake, he knelt at the dog's side, talking softly to calm him and reassure him, while he examined the spring and how best to release it. "I know, I know, fella, but you're going to have to relax...I know... Goddamn it! Just let me get a grip on the blasted thing...whoa, Barny. Stay down."

His brown eyes wide and pained yet trusting, Barny remained still long enough for Skye to manhandle the trap and force it open. Reflexively, the dog pulled out his paw, but screamed again with pain when he tried to scramble to his feet and put his weight upon it. Skye disarmed the trap and threw it aside in disgust, then took the dog in his arms.

"Down, boy," he said again, more gently. "Lie down and let me get a look at that."

It was bad. There was profuse bleeding from the deep, jagged wounds where the teeth of the trap had penetrated, and Skye suspected also that the foreleg had been fractured from the enormous force of the closing trap. To make matters worse, the dog was already drenched from the snow, which would exacerbate shock, and there was no way he was going to be able to walk back to the road.

I'll have to carry him, Skye realized. If I can, he amended, as Barny had filled out considerably in the past few months and must weigh sixty or seventy pounds by now.

It was then that Skye felt the first pricking of concern. He wasn't sure how far away the Jeep was. He hadn't really been hunting today, he'd been sulking.

Which meant he'd been out of touch with the forest, the birds and the weather, which had turned positively nasty. The snow was swirling in the air around them, tossed on a powerful wind. Visibility had been cut considerably and would be diminished more if the storm's intensity increased. He hadn't even listened to a weather report before venturing out. He couldn't think of an occasion when he had ever been so careless.

"I screwed up, Barny," he said as he applied pressure to the wounds, hoping to stop the bleeding. "But don't worry. I'll get you out of here."

Right, he thought grimly. How?

Holly watched the snow fall, feeling increasingly worried. Skye ought to have been home by now. The snow had been heavy for several hours, and he surely wouldn't have stayed out in it. On the other hand, considering the mood in which he had left...it was impossible to predict what he would do.

She tried to remember how he had been dressed when he'd left. Certainly not in foul weather gear. Was he warm enough? Dry enough? Did he have anything to eat or drink? The wretched storm was turning into a blizzard. What if he was lost?

Don't be silly, she ordered herself. He's an outdoorsman who's been doing this all his life. He's far too experienced to get into trouble. He's probably sitting in a nice, warm bar somewhere, drowning his sorrows in an amber glass of whiskey.

She ruined her fingernails, chewing on them, nevertheless.

By the time there was only a couple of hours of daylight left, Holly was frantic. Her own concerns about getting away to think things over had vanished as her fears for her husband escalated. She had begun to imagine all sorts of dreadful things.

She tried meditating to calm herself, but its effects only lasted a few minutes. Back in a normal state of consciousness, anxiety assaulted her again.

She wandered into the greenhouse, among her herbs and plants, her safe place, the place where she had always been comforted and serene. Gently she brushed their leaves, trying to empty her mind. She would miss these plants if she left. They'd established themselves nicely here in her greenhouse...who was going to care for them if she were gone?

Find him, a voice deep inside her said. *He needs you. You must go out and find him.*

He doesn't need me, she tried to assure herself. The man is completely self-sufficient. Besides I haven't the slightest idea where he is. On our property alone, there are miles of fields and forest in which to hunt.

Go out and look for him.

The voice was insistent, and Holly trusted her intuition enough to pay attention. Something was definitely wrong.

Go out and look for him.

Okay, smart stuff. Where?

It struck her that she could search for his Jeep. If she found it, she would know what part of the wilderness he had entered. Besides, the Jeep was equipped with a police radio. Maybe the sheriff's office could pinpoint its location electronically.

Buoyed by this thought, Holly hurried inside to call Skye's office and alert them to the possibility that he might be missing in the storm. But when she picked up the receiver, she got no dial tone. Looking out the front window, she saw the limb from the oak tree that had fallen on the telephone wire, knocking it to the ground.

Terrific. Find the Jeep. Okay. But there were several roads to search, and she didn't know where to begin. With the snow falling and the hours of daylight limited, she would have to narrow it down somehow. Had he gone into the fields or into the forest?

Holly went into Skye's office and opened his glass-fronted gun cabinet. Four of the five weapons that were kept there remained. Thoughts of Willy flashed, and she felt dizzy. Get a grip, for God's sake, she ordered herself.

The 12-gauge, with the bigger barrel and the bigger shells, was for shooting pheasant, a relatively large bird. There were two 12-gauge, double-barrel shotguns in the case.

One of the other weapons was not a shotgun at all— it was some sort of automatic rifle. Police issue, no doubt. Not a hunter's gun.

The last gun in the case looked old and beautiful, a gun that she, as a girl, would have longed to possess herself. It had only a single barrel, which was the same diameter as the other two. Another 12-gauge. Which meant the missing weapon was Skye's 20-gauge shotgun. It had a narrower barrel and was used for shooting smaller birds. Like grouse.

She remembered what he'd told her—grouse hunting was usually conducted on hilly terrain. Forests, woodlands. If he had stayed on their own property—a likely, though not an absolute, possibility—there were only a few areas where he could be. And she believed she knew the road accesses to all of them.

The snow was still coming down heavily when Holly backed her Camry out of the driveway on her quest to find Skye. She found herself wishing he'd left her the Jeep, which would have been more reliable in this weather. She wasn't very confident about driving in the snow. Down in Arizona, she hadn't had much practice.

She silently gave thanks that at least the car had front-wheel drive. But her palms were slick because her husband was in trouble and there wasn't much time.

Sweating with exertion and weariness, Skye stumbled, falling to one knee in the deepening snow. He managed to keep hold of Barny, whom he was cradling in his arms. The dog whimpered loudly, a sound that, although it wrenched Skye's heart, reassured him that the animal was at least still conscious.

Gently, he set the dog down, speaking softly to him. Barny kept trying to lick his injured leg, which had swollen to twice its normal diameter and must have hurt like hell.

Skye climbed to his feet and tried to get his bearings, but it was difficult to recognize any landmarks. The poor visibility combined with the snow-shrouding of trees and bushes to make everything look the same. He could only estimate, from the time he'd been hiking, that he'd come at least half the distance back to the road where he'd left the Jeep. Assuming, of course, that he'd been traveling in the right direction, which was probably a poor assumption. The snowfall had obscured the trail—which he hadn't exactly been sticking to in the first place.

He was exhausted, his back and shoulders aching from the weight of the dog, his legs leaden. Worse, although he'd felt hot while tramping, it took only a couple of minutes of standing still in the wind for him to start feeling bitterly cold. At least the wind had been behind him on the hike—that was the only mercy. If they'd had to walk straight into it, they probably wouldn't have gotten this far.

Barny stopped worrying about his leg and curled up into a tight ball. He was shivering. Skye pushed up a sodden sleeve to examine the misted face of his watch. Less than an hour of daylight left—if you could call this snow-gloom daylight. Not enough time, he didn't think, to find his way out of here before conditions *really* got bad.

"Guess it's time for Plan Number Two, Barny, old boy," he said aloud. The dog lifted his head to the sound of his master's voice, a good sign. "We gotta get ourselves into some shelter. See any caves around here, fella? Or maybe a nice big boulder slanted so it has an overhang? We find something like that and we can make ourselves a nice little hut. You stay here, boy. I'm going to scout around.''

As soon as the dog perceived that his master was leaving him, he let out a piercing series of yelps that didn't stop even as Skye pitched his voice to its more reassuring tones. "I'm not leaving you, Barny. No way I'm leaving you. No, boy, stay. Good dog. Stay. You usually do the sniffing around for me, but now I'm doing it for you. Watch me. I'm moving in a circle, I'm keeping an eye on you. I'm hunting for a downed tree, or a large rock, or anything that we can use as a buffer against the wind. Take it easy, Barny. I'm trying to save your life.''

The yelps devolved into whines of pain that tore at Skye's heart. It's all my fault, as usual, he was thinking wearily. Me, the big hunter, the skilled woodsman, storming out into a goddamn blizzard, not even bringing any gear. Smart Rawlins. Real, goddamn sensible.

"I deserve to freeze," he called to Barny. "But you don't, dammit, so keep your chin up. I'm going to get us both out of this mess, don't worry.''

I'll do the worrying for both of us, he added silently.

Holly couldn't believe her luck. She'd found the Jeep at the second spot she had tried. It was parked in a hollow on the side of the road near an area that Skye had once pointed out to her as the best damn ruffed grouse hunting territory on her grandfather's property. She would have tried here first, if there hadn't been a somewhat closer place to check.

Trouble was, there was no sign of Skye or Barny. Any tracks they might have left had long since been obliterated by the falling snow.

Holly climbed into the Jeep, which was covered by nearly six inches of snow, and stuck her key into the ignition. It started sluggishly. She hammered on its loud horn. Her elation at having successfully located the Jeep was beginning to fade as other thoughts crowded in. Why hadn't Skye returned to his vehicle? Was he lost in the woods? Injured? Had there been some sort of hunting accident? Her mind shied away from the last possibility.

Quickly, she switched on the police radio, sighing with relief when it lit up and started buzzing. She took the microphone and, after a few false starts, figured out how to use it. She got through to one of the deputies whom she had met once or twice, explained the situation and gave him her location.

The deputy, a laconic man whom Skye had told her was barely competent to do his job, informed her that both the town's cruisers and their single ambulance were out on the highway trying to clean up a major accident, with personal injury. It would be at least an hour, maybe more, before anybody could get to her.

"But it'll be dark by then, and Skye's lost in the woods," she protested.

"Are you sure?" the deputy asked, treating her as if she were a hysterical housewife. "I've never known

Rawlins to get lost in the woods. Most husbands, you know, when they don't come home exactly on time, are down at the local bar, getting away from it all—"

"Listen, you jackass, your boss is in trouble, and if you don't get some help out here in record time, it's going to mean your job. Do you understand me?"

"I'll send someone out as soon as I can, but I'm telling you, ma'am, there just ain't anybody right now to go."

"Well, find somebody!" she cried in frustration and signed off.

Jumping out of the Jeep, she shaded her eyes against the driving snow and gazed into the woods. The wind was roaring out of the forest, striking her head-on. The trees were ghostly, and all evidence of any woodland trails was buried under several inches of snow.

Now what? she wondered. Miles of upland forest swept away from this spot. He was out there, yes. But she couldn't count on help from the police, at least not yet. She was going to have to find him herself.

A particularly strong gust of wind assaulted her, bringing with it the faint but unmistakable cry of an animal in pain. Barny? Was he injured? Was that why they hadn't made it back to the Jeep?

The rational part of her mind protested that it was impossible to recognize the dog's cry at a distance, in a blizzard. But when the sound came again, she was certain. It was Barny, and something had happened to him.

She delayed only long enough to search the Jeep for supplies. If the dog was injured, they would need— what?—a blanket. She found one tossed in the back along with an old windbreaker and a filthy pair of leather gloves. She collected them all. From the glove compartment she took a flashlight, a first-aid kit and an ancient box of raisins.

There was another blanket in the trunk of her car, which she also gathered up. Now that she was out here, she could think of several things she wished she had brought from home, including a complete stock of herbal medicines. She recalled, though, that she had a couple of useful tinctures thrust in the bottom of her pocketbook.

Unfolding one of the blankets, she dumped her hastily collected gear in the middle, her handbag included, and wrapped it into a bundle, which she flung across her back. It was heavy. She adjusted it as comfortably as she could, hoping the trek would not be too long. The cry of pain echoed again, from the same direction . . . slightly to the right of the Jeep. How far away? she wondered. The wind could carry sound a long distance. It could confuse the direction of the sound, too, she knew, especially in a storm.

She would have to trust her instincts, as she had so far, and hope to heaven she wasn't making a horrible mistake. If she miscalculated, there would be three of them lost in the forest this evening.

Where's the strong and passionate earth goddess, afraid of nothing, who danced her way into my heart?

Here she is, Skye. She's coming.

Jerking the hood of her jacket as far down over her face as she could manage, Holly plunged into the woods.

Thirteen

The shelter Skye had located was in a small clearing in the woods, in the lee of an old uprooted tree. Its ample root ball, fallen in such a direction as to cut off the most bitter blasts of wind, was roughly circular and a good six feet in diameter. It was tilted in such a way to allow one to scrunch down under it and have something of a roof over one's head and body. He added to this effect by hacking off several sturdy evergreen branches from the surrounding trees and filling in the empty spots on the root ball.

"It ain't much, Barny, but it's home," he said, after making the dog a soft nest of dry leaves and pine and getting him in underneath the shelter. "You rest now. I gotta see about building us a fire."

Using his bare hands, which had gone past cold to numb, Skye hollowed out a circular well in the snow in front of the shelter. On a flat rock nearby, he laid out what minimal gear he had stowed in his hunting vest and pockets: two 20-gauge shotgun shells—he'd only grabbed a few on his way out of the house. One Swiss army knife complete with various small tools, none of which were especially useful at this moment. One snakebite kit, never used. One tin of gun oil. One topographic map of the Big Horn River area of Montana, a couple hours' drive east of here. One duck-call whistle that had never worked. One battered compass. One can of waterproof matches. One ancient, white-tinged chocolate bar. One scrunched-up ten dollar bill.

Skye restowed everything except the matches, the map, the ten-spot. He hesitated over the candy bar, the very sight of which sent hunger pangs shooting through him, but decided he might require its energy later on. Besides, he was loath to eat something that Barny couldn't, and a lot of dogs were hypersensitive to chocolate.

Next he gathered wood, deliberately choosing the types that were most resistant to damp and snow. He stripped a dead birch of its bark for kindling, using that, together with the ten dollar bill and the topographic map to get his fire started. As he built it, he remembered Holly's fire in the forest on the night they'd made love. In the Native American way, she had called out to the spirits of the four directions—

east, north, south, and west—to come and feed the fire.

What the hell, Skye figured. I need all the help I can get. He asked for the spirits' assistance, as well. "Blessed be," he said self-consciously.

As the fire caught, smoking excessively from the damp kindling, hissing as the snowflakes fell into its flame, Skye visualized Holly as she had been on that magical night. Her thick black hair. Her multicolored skirt, curving over slender hips and long, long legs. Her lovely, entranced face, eyes dreamy, mouth soft. Her sexy, husky voice chanting the words of magic, of power. Such a strong woman in so many ways. Honest, courageous and full of love and laughter. Yet holding within her such darkness. She'd had knowledge of, and intimacy with, the most vicious forms of evil. Of course she was hurt, of course she was scarred. Yet there must be a way, he thought miserably, of bringing her out of that darkness and into the light.

You could give up hunting, a voice inside him said.

Don't be ridiculous. I've done it all my life.

But you do injure, you do kill. You're sitting here, agonizing over your wounded dog, but you shed no tears over the birds whose lives you've ended.

It's not their deaths I seek. It's the chase I love, the process, the game of wits—city-softened man versus wild creature of nature. It takes me back in time, in spirit, just as ceremonial fire building and chanting does for her. It's my way of participating in an ancient, sacred rite.

At the expense of innocent creatures' lives? Sometimes, for love, you have to make a sacrifice.

Maybe. But, even for love, can you deny who you are?

Skye shook himself. Despite the warmth of the fire, he was getting dozy. A bad sign. The fire, the shelter weren't enough. The cold was getting to him.

He had only his jacket to keep him warm, and Barny had only his thick golden coat. At night, in this kind of weather, it wasn't enough. If they were going to survive, he was going to have to fashion a better shelter. A snow hut maybe, with snow itself providing the necessary insulation against the blizzard outside. A good idea but, damn, he was so numb, so weary. Maybe if he took just a little nap, he'd feel refreshed and able to get to work... Just a short one. Forty winks. Stupid thing to do, of course, any woodsman would know better, but...

The wolf lurked in the shadows, downwind from the clearing. He scented blood, which excited him. The heavy, wet snow had dampened his desire for hunting, but the smell aroused his hunger. It had been several hours since he'd eaten, and the cold, white blanket that cloaked the forest had driven all his usual prey into their deepest hiding spots.

Cautiously, he advanced toward the clearing. The wind brought him the acrid smell of smoke, which made him shake his nose with distaste. He feared smoke and the fire that caused it, and he'd been scavenging long enough to know that the fires were some-

*times ringed with rocks and tended by those big, two-
legged creatures that he feared even more than fire.*

*But he'd also learned that the big, two-legged crea-
tures often kept food near their tiny, contained fires.
And that it was easier to snatch an already dead piece
of meat than to bring down a deer. It didn't taste as
good—he'd much rather swallow hot, freshly killed,
bloody meat—but he was cold and he needed to con-
serve his strength, especially now that the white, wet
stuff was covering the earth.*

*The smell of blood was stronger now. His darting
yellow eyes told him why: a wounded animal lay in the
clearing, hiding from him underneath a fallen tree. A
large animal, one he wouldn't usually attack because
it would mean a fight. He would win, of course, he
always did. In this case, he would win easily. The animal was injured.*

*Another smell drifted toward him over the blood
and the smoke. It made him stop; it nearly made him
run. One of the big, two-legged creatures was hiding
there, as well. But he was still, not moving. Was he injured, too? Weakened, yes, the wolf sensed. Not as
dangerous as usual. Maybe not dangerous at all.*

*The wolf stood poised, watching, waiting. A good
hunter knew how to bide his time.*

Barny shifted and whined loudly, jerking Skye up-
right and alert. Christ, I almost lost it, he thought,
really frightened now. What the hell's the matter with
me?

He checked the dog, aware that his cry had sounded less like a whine of pain than a whine of alarm. Barny's head was up, his ears cocked. Did he hear something? Or was he smart enough to register alarm at the sight of his master falling asleep in a blizzard?

Actually, the snowfall seemed to have let up a bit. Maybe even stopped. It was difficult to be certain in the semidarkness, with the way the wind was blowing the stuff around. He hoped it was stopping. That would make things marginally easier.

He rose, stretching his cold, numb limbs. Gotta move, gotta do jumping jacks, for Crissake, gotta do something to get warm. Gotta shore up this shelter somehow—with saplings, maybe, and with leaves and dirt and snow. Snow's an excellent insulator. A clever woodsman uses what he's got, and what he's got here is lots and lots of snow.

When he climbed out of the shelter, Skye loaded his shotgun and took it with him, with the vague notion of hunting something—a jackrabbit maybe—for supper. The long hike with Barny on his shoulders had thoroughly depleted his energy reserves. He had a fire; he could cook.

The fire wasn't looking too healthy at the moment, though. Needed more wood. Some logs, if possible. Skye dusted off the flat rock near the fire and put the gun down. "Be right back, Barny," he reassured his dog. "Gotta find us some firewood."

Barny whined and made as if to get up. "Stay," Skye ordered him sharply. "Good boy. You guard the campsite. I'll be back soon."

Barny sniffed the air and whined again.

* * *

The wolf watched the two-legged creature move away from the fire. He vanished into the woods on the most distant side of the clearing. The wolf's tongue came out, licking his pointed teeth. The wounded animal sensed his presence—whined, sniffed the air, tried to move. Along with his blood, the wolf could scent his fear.

Now was the moment. The more dangerous of the two creatures was gone. Now was the time to move, to lunge, to hunt. To taste the lovely, hot flavor of fresh-killed meat.

Bogged down in knee-high snow and fighting a head-on wind that tore her breath away, Holly was about to give up and try to find her way back to the Jeep when she smelled smoke. She had screamed herself hoarse, yelling for Skye, but there had been no answering call. Not surprisingly, since she was shouting into the wind.

But the scent of smoke was strong, and in the gathering darkness ahead, she thought she caught sight of a flicker of red. "Skye!" she cried again.

There was no reply, but surely that was a fire—not much of one, it looked like sputtering coals instead of cheerful flames—but what could one expect in this weather? The snow had let up, though. Thank goodness for that.

She was struggling toward it when she heard, much

more loudly now, the pathetic whimper of a frightened dog. Barny.

She had found them! They hadn't heard her or seen her. Approaching from downwind, she had effectively hunted them, her unsuspecting prey.

Running now, as best she could in these conditions, she plunged through the brush and thickets, up a slope and over a rise... and abruptly stopped. Yes, there was a fire and beyond it, a makeshift shelter of sorts. She could see no sign of Skye. But there was a vicious dog standing stiff outside the shelter, growling, looking ready to attack... not an injured dog, surely... not a dog at all.

It was a huge, gray, hungry-looking wolf.

She'd found the camp. But a deadly predator had found it first.

Fourteen

"Skye!" Holly screamed, only to have the wind blow the word back into her face. But the wolf either heard or smelled her, for its head came around and its yellow eyes nailed her in the gathering darkness.

Holly dropped her bundle and froze. She heard the growl. And saw, at the same time, Barny struggle to his feet in the shelter, and reengage the wolf's attention with a ferocious growl of his own. He limped out of the shelter and backed away from the fire, away from her, growling some more, plainly trying to distract the wolf from the unarmed human morsel whom he could see cowering on the other side of the clearing. He was injured, yet he was trying to protect her.

Oh, God, it was working. With a cautious look over his shoulder, the wolf followed Barny, moving farther and farther away from her, away from the fire.

All Holly could think of at that moment was her own beloved pet of so many years ago. Dusty, whom another predator had threatened to mutilate and kill. And all she could see was the flat rock beside the fire and upon it, Skye's shotgun.

She ran forward, reached the rock, grabbed the gun. She broke it open. Both barrels were loaded. She raised it to her shoulder in a motion she hadn't practiced for more than a decade, but which she had not, it seemed, forgotten. The wolf, attracted by her motion, had circled and crouched, but he had not yet run. Barny circled the other way, leaving her a clear shot.

Holly aimed for the ground at the wolf's feet. All she could do was frighten him. Bird shot might injure, but certainly wouldn't kill an animal of this size.

She released the safety then pulled the forward trigger, exploding the shell in the right barrel. She heard the boom and felt the kick of the stock, but she continued to hold it steady. The wolf leaped into the air, then turned tail and dashed for the shelter of the woods. Holly pulled the second trigger to convince him not to venture back here again.

"Nice shooting," said a voice behind her.

She swung around to find Skye standing a few feet behind her, his arms full of firewood, blinking at her through snow-encrusted eyelids, as if he didn't quite trust what he was seeing. But when, with a sigh of great thankfulness and relief she put down the gun and opened her arms, Skye shook his head as if to clear it, then dropped his load of wood and walked straight into her embrace.

The search party found them a little more than an hour later. Led by Skye's friend Jake, two off-duty sheriff's deputies and several volunteers had found the Jeep at the location Holly had radioed in and followed her tracks through the newly fallen snow. Holly was delighted to see them, although Skye expressed what she could only assume was feigned dismay.

"We've got a great fire going, and we've been shoring up our shelter with dirt and rocks, saplings and melted, refrozen snow. Holly smeared some of her herbal concoctions on Barny's leg and found us some edible mushrooms from under the snow. Hell, we had a cozy little spot here, complete with blankets and freshly scented pine, where we were all set to spend a restful night, but you boys just had to interrupt."

"You'll be spending a restful night, all right," Jake informed him. "In the hospital."

But as it turned out, the hospital wasn't necessary for any of them. Even Barny was sent home by the vet to recuperate, his left paw stitched and immobilized in a cast. Neither Skye nor Holly had suffered any ill effects from their adventure that rest, blankets and plenty of hot herbal tea couldn't cure. But their friends and rescuers wanted to hear all the details of ordeal, and it was close to midnight before everyone left and Skye and Holly had the house to themselves.

They were sitting in the living room on a sofa in front of the roaring fire that Jake had built on the hearth. Skye was leaning against the arm at one end, and Holly was a couple of feet away from him, near the other arm. He stretched his hand along the sofa back and beckoned with his fingers.

"Come a little closer, Annie Oakley."

She turned a grave face to him. "I would have shot him, you know. If he hadn't run. If he'd continued to attack Barny, I would have shot him dead."

Skye listened, but kept his mouth shut.

"I didn't think I had it in me," she went on. "It was instant, automatic. Some sort of reflex that ordered me to take up the shotgun to defend a creature I loved."

"There's nothing wrong with that, Holly. In fact, it's about as human a reaction as I can imagine."

"I kept thinking, what if you'd been the one injured and helpless and that wolf had been attacking you."

"There'd be a certain rough justice to that," he said with a grin. "The hunter becomes the hunted."

"I'd have blown his head off."

"Tough, with bird shot," Skye said lightly, then saw from her expression that this was not a laughing matter. And the meaning of what she'd said began to sink in.

He swallowed hard. "Are you trying to tell me something, Holly?"

She nodded, looking away from him into the fire, her black hair partially covering her face.

He leaned forward, caught her wrist and pulled her toward him. She pushed her hair aside, and on her face Skye saw a smile so radiant that he was momentarily dazzled. "So say it. I want to hear it, whatever it is."

"I love you, Skye."

He leaned back. "You want to run that by me once again?"

She raised her eyebrows and crept a little closer on the sofa. "I love you."

"You love me?"

"Yes."

"Evil hunter that I am?"

"Yes."

"Unreformed, never-likely-to-be-rehabilitated killer of small birds and animals?"

"Yes."

He sighed. "You still going to Salt Lake City?"

"No."

"Still want a divorce?"

"No."

"You want to stay here, you and me, living on your grandfather's land?"

"Yes."

"Forever?"

"Yes."

"Forsaking all others, till death do us part?"

"Mm-hmm. Absolutely."

Skye closed his eyes. "What about the past? What about Willy Hess?"

"He's dead. He's really, truly, dead at last." She bit her lip, then tried to explain. "It's as if he were that wolf. A predator, preying on the weak, the defenseless. And when it came right down to it, I felt no compunction about shooting at him." Her voice softened. "Of course, I like wolves, usually. They mate for life, did you know that? They're beautiful animals."

"Yeah," Skye agreed. "Let's not insult the wolf by comparing Willy to him."

"You're right. The wolf was doing what was natural to wolves...what he needs to do in order to survive. What Willy was doing was unnatural, evil and sick."

She paused, then added, "I think I've always felt guilty somehow. Because he was my brother. I guess I thought there must have been something I could have done to help him. I've even wondered whether it was my fault...whether I'd unknowingly said or done something, when we were very young, that twisted him and set him on his path. But now I see it was his choice, his responsibility. Willy got what he deserved."

"Amen to that."

"I've felt like a victim for so long," she added, letting out a deep breath. "The only time I've felt truly strong and powerful has been outside, in the forest, gathering my herbs or dancing around the sacred fire. But this evening when Barny was in danger, I discovered that I wasn't a victim anymore. I could and did take action. And, somehow, it's freed me. Willy Hess won't haunt me any longer."

"Come here," said Skye.

She scooted over.

He hugged her close for a moment, then leaned away again. "So much for Willy. Now me. I want you to look at me. Really look at me."

She did so, gravely, her head tilted a little to one side.

"What do you see?" he asked her.

She grinned. Reaching out, she tweaked his mustache. "I see a handsome man, a little rough and rugged around the edges, perhaps, but I like that. It's sexy."

"Um. What else?"

"I see an understanding and generous man with a ten-gallon heart."

"Even better. Anything else?"

"I see the face of the hunter I love," she said gently. "It's a face I hope I'll always see, on the pillows at night, at the breakfast table in the morning and over the heads of our children someday, God willing."

He tried to pull her in and kiss her, but she resisted. "Just a second. There's one other thing." She was studying his face carefully, considering every line, every angle.

"Well?"

"I can see now that I was mistaken. You don't really resemble him at all."

This time he pulled harder, and she came. They kissed with great tenderness at first, then hotly, ardently. She shifted, trying to stretch out full length on the sofa with him beside her.

But he said, "Wait."

"What?"

Taking her hand, he rose and pulled her to her feet. She thought he was taking her upstairs, but instead he led her closer to the fire. Opening the grate, he piled on some logs. Then he pressed a switch on the tape deck and coming from the speakers, Holly heard the sensuous Native American music she had played for him that night in the woods.

He walked back to her, stopping less than a yard away. "And so, witch lady, would you care to dance?"

"I'd like that very much."

"First, will you do something for me?"

"Anything."

He grinned mischievously. "Skyclad, Holly. I want you to dance skyclad. That's how the real goddesses do it, I believe."

"Only," she said slowly, "when they have a partner with whom they mean to share their energy. The god who is the consort must display himself in all his naked glory, also."

"That," he said, jerking off his sweater and ripping at the buttons on his shirt, "is a small price to pay for the pleasure of seeing my goddess revealed."

There was no one to touch him for pure, rugged, masculine grace, she thought as Skye stripped down to his skin and advanced toward her to help her remove her garments, as well. It seemed natural—playful and innocent, even—to watch her clothing melt away under his quick, knowing hands and to emerge naked in the firelight.

She could feel his electric blue eyes admiring her body. Smiling, she pirouetted, affording him a better view, while at the same time she took in the full glory of his well-proportioned body with its broad shoulders, gently sculpted muscles, flat belly and lean hips. And of course, his manhood, rising to attention now as they began to dance. Centuries of pagan ritual drifted through her mind—the maypole planted into the fertile earth, the chalice and the blade.

The dance started slowly, but soon the quickening tempo of the music urged them on to greater and greater heights of movement and excitement. They faced each other, a few feet apart, mirroring each other's motions, linked by eye and mind. Holly's hair came loose and fell about her shoulders, and she felt a cleansing perspiration flower on her skin at the precise moment that she saw the sheen of sweat break out on Skye.

Breathing deeply from her belly, she centered herself deep in the lower chakras where the generative powers flow, feeling the life-giving energy circle. The creative principle, powerful and real, spinning like a wheel, faster and faster, tighter and tighter, with ever more dazzling light.

When they came together, irresistibly, both rushing forward at the same moment, they laughed and tumbled to the floor, finding what little comfort they required in the rough texture of a woven Navajo hearth rug. Skye's big body pinned her with his delicious weight, his hands skimmed her body lightly, then gave her the deeper, more violent caresses she needed and desired. His kisses were molten, his breathless urgings raw and wild.

This was not a gentle mating, nor did she wish it so. This was as wildly primitive as the first great coupling that had created the heavens and the earth.

"Yes," she panted. "Now!" She arched her hips upward to meet his descending thrust. Then they were one, and the shock of recognition jolted Holly's soul. How could she have doubted it for even one moment? This man was her forever lover. He was the true mate of her soul.

Later, much later, after moving back up to the sofa where they cuddled together, still nude, gazing into the glowing fire, Skye cocked his head to one side and asked her, "What are you grinning about?"

"I was thinking about my grandfather. Wondering what he would say if he could see us now."

"Well, I reckon he'd be tickled pink."

"You know, it's strange. In general, he was a terrible judge of character. But he turned out to be right about you. And right about our marriage."

"All I can say is, I sure never expected, during all those great hunting and fishing expeditions we took together, that my good buddy Tom would stick me with a bride."

"But you're glad we took the honorable course and kept our deathbed promise to him?"

Skye grinned. "Do I look like I'm glad?"

"You look naked and disreputable, Sheriff Rawlins."

"Oh, yeah? Look lower."

"You've got to be kidding."

"Suppose we go upstairs to bed, Mrs. Rawlins. The next time I discharge my weapon, I'd like it to be in more comfortable surroundings."

Holly jumped up and ran toward the stairs. "You'll have to find me first," she laughed over her shoulder. "And with Barny incapacitated, you won't be able to cheat this time."

He rose to follow. "There's nothing a hunter likes better than a challenging pursuit."

"Come catch me then."

"I'm right behind you, fire lady, queen of night."

She led him straight to her bed. Which was exactly where, Skye decided, he wanted to spend his nights for at least the next fifty years.

"I love you, Skye Rawlins," she whispered.

"Blessed be," he quietly replied.

*   *   *   *   *

SILHOUETTE® Desire®

THEY'RE HOT...
THEY'RE COOL...
THEY'RE ALL-AMERICAN GUYS...
THEY'RE RED, WHITE AND BLUE HEROES

Zeke #793 by Annette Broadrick *(Man of the Month)*
Ben #794 by Karen Leabo
Derek #795 by Leslie Davis Guccione
Cameron #796 by Beverly Barton
Jake #797 by Helen R. Myers
Will #798 by Kelly Jamison

Look for these six red-blooded, white-knight, blue-collar men
Coming your way next month
Only from Silhouette Desire

SDRWB-A

OFFICIAL RULES • MILLION DOLLAR BIG WIN SWEEPSTAKES
NO PURCHASE OR OBLIGATION NECESSARY TO ENTER

To enter, follow the directions published. **ALTERNATE MEANS OF ENTRY:** Hand-print your name and address on a 3"×5" card and mail to either: Silhouette Big Win, 3010 Walden Ave., P.O. Box 1867, Buffalo, NY 14269-1867, or Silhouette Big Win, P.O. Box 609, Fort Erie, Ontario L2A 5X3, and we will assign your Sweepstakes numbers (Limit: one entry per envelope). For eligibility, entries must be received no later than March 31, 1994 and be sent via 1st-class mail. No liability is assumed for printing errors or lost, late or misdirected entries.

To determine winners, the sweepstakes numbers on submitted entries will be compared against a list of randomly preselected prizewinning numbers. In the event all prizes are not claimed via the return of prizewinning numbers, random drawings will be held from among all other entries received to award unclaimed prizes.

Prizewinners will be determined no later than May 30, 1994. Selection of winning numbers and random drawings are under the supervision of D.L. Blair, Inc., an independent judging organization whose decisions are final. One prize to a family or organization. No substitution will be made for any prize, except as offered. Taxes and duties on all prizes are the sole responsibility of winners. Winners will be notified by mail. Chances of winning are determined by the number of entries distributed and received.

Sweepstakes open to persons 18 years of age or older, except employees and immediate family members of Torstar Corporation, D.L. Blair, Inc., their affiliates, subsidiaries and all other agencies, entities and persons connected with the use, marketing or conduct of this Sweepstakes. All applicable laws and regulations apply. Sweepstakes offer void wherever prohibited by law. Any litigation within the province of Quebec respecting the conduct and awarding of a prize in this Sweepstakes must be submitted to the Régies des Loteries et Courses du Quebec. In order to win a prize, residents of Canada will be required to correctly answer a time-limited arithmetical skill-testing question. Values of all prizes are in U.S. currency.

Winners of major prizes will be obligated to sign and return an affidavit of eligibility and release of liability within 30 days of notification. In the event of non-compliance within this time period, prize may be awarded to an alternate winner. Any prize or prize notification returned as undeliverable will result in the awarding of the prize to an alternate winner. By acceptance of their prize, winners consent to use of their names, photographs or other likenesses for purposes of advertising, trade and promotion on behalf of Torstar Corporation without further compensation, unless prohibited by law.

This Sweepstakes is presented by Torstar Corporation, its subsidiaries and affiliates in conjunction with book, merchandise and/or product offerings. Prizes are as follows: Grand Prize—$1,000,000 (payable at $33,333.33 a year for 30 years). First through Sixth Prizes may be presented in different creative executions, each with the following approximate values: First Prize—$35,000; Second Prize—$10,000; 2 Third Prizes—$5,000 each; 5 Fourth Prizes—$1,000 each; 10 Fifth Prizes—$250 each; 1,000 Sixth Prizes—$100 each. Prizewinners will have the opportunity of selecting any prize offered for that level. A travel-prize option if offered and selected by winner, must be completed within 12 months of selection and is subject to hotel and flight accommodations availability. Torstar Corporation may present this sweepstakes utilizing names other than Million Dollar Sweepstakes. For a current list of all prize options offered within prize levels and all names the Sweepstakes may utilize, send a self-addressed stamped envelope (WA residents need not affix return postage) to: Million Dollar Sweepstakes Prize Options/Names, P.O. Box 7410, Blair, NE 68009.

For a list of prizewinners (available after July 31, 1994) send a separate, stamped self-addressed envelope to: Million Dollar Sweepstakes Winners, P.O. Box 4728, Blair NE 68009.

SWPS693

INTIMATE MOMENTS®

10TH
Anniversary

Celebrate our anniversary with a fabulous collection of firsts....

The first Intimate Moments titles written by three of your favorite authors:

NIGHT MOVES   **Heather Graham Pozzessere**
LADY OF THE NIGHT   **Emilie Richards**
A STRANGER'S SMILE **Kathleen Korbel**

Silhouette Intimate Moments is proud to present a FREE hardbound collection of our authors' firsts—titles that you will treasure in the years to come, from some of the line's founding writers.

This collection will not be sold in retail stores and is available only through this exclusive offer. Look for details in Silhouette Intimate Moments titles available in retail stores in May, June and July.

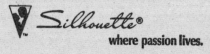